Sherlock Holmes
at the Varieties

Sherlock Holmes
at the Varieties

Val Andrews

**BREESE
BOOKS
LONDON**

First published in 2000 by
Breese Books Ltd
164 Kensington Park Road, London W11 2ER, England

© Breese Books Ltd, 2000

ISBN: 0 947533 82 6

Front cover photograph is reproduced by kind permission of
Retrograph Archive, London

Typeset in 11½/14pt Caslon by
Ann Buchan (Typesetters), Middlesex
Printed and bound in Great Britain by
Itchen Printers Ltd, Southampton

CHAPTER ONE

The House on the Green

The miraculous reappearance of my friend Mr Sherlock Holmes (which I have documented in my account *The Adventure of the Empty House*), brightened my life considerably, especially when I was able to return to the old rooms at Baker Street. It was not just a question of resuming old ways for I took genuine delight in spending time once more with Holmes himself. My way of life before his then tragic disappearance had been somewhat bizarre by most standards. Being a widower with but a single friend had been fair enough, but when that single companion had been removed from my everyday life, life itself tended to become a mere existence. Of course, there had been my medical work, but no social life whatever, for my association with Holmes tended to remove me from any sort of the usual friendly circle or crowd. Of course, after his disappearance I had looked up a few old friends but found their conversation hardly inspiring and their activities, which might once have delighted me, were no longer those in which I wished to participate. Sherlock Holmes had made me aware of the pointless nature of hunting and shooting, and I no longer enjoyed house parties.

So, you see, when my friend unaccountably returned, it was not just my joy, but my salvation. The game was afoot once more, thanks to the resurrection of the world's first, and greatest, private detective. Slowly, at first, we recommenced those activities which we had both enjoyed in the halcyon days, outside of Holmes's professional work. Pleasant meals at Simpson's, brisk walks in Regent's Park and dreamy evenings, transported by musical recitals, at the Royal Albert Hall. I was also able to enjoy Holmes's impromptu renditions of obscure violin pieces, some of which were obscure because they were impromptu through composition as well as execution!

Of course, Holmes, as of yore, had his black days, but seemed either to have forsaken, or else better controlled, those intemperate addictions of the old days.

Mrs Hudson had been particularly delighted by his return and it took many months before she slowed down upon daily culinary celebration. 'Oh I know, Mr Holmes, you did say you only wanted a little something, but it does give me such pleasure to see you and the doctor seated there with one of my veal pies standing steaming between you!'

As for Sherlock Holmes himself, he seemed quickly able to resume both his career and mode of living, calming our repeated thanksgivings as well he could. He did not affect to be casual about his dramatic return, he really was. But in one respect he seemed to have mellowed a little, seeming able to give me rather more consideration than before.

One evening, some twelve months after the restoration, he remarked to me, 'Watson, my dear fellow, in all the years of our association I have never asked you if there was anywhere you might wish us to go, quite taking for granted that our tastes conspired. Whilst you have never protested and have seemed happy to follow my lead, you have been inclined sometimes to nod off during recitals. It occurs to me that we should really take it in turns to suggest some form of diversion for our free evenings. For all I know, you might wish to play tennis or learn to render upon the French horn. Tonight, I suggest you choose. I know of course that you were fond of going to Maskelyne's in your student days which indicates a taste for light entertainment that I do not altogether share. I know, for instance, that you were also fond of the music hall and visited at least one such establishment on a fairly regular basis.'

I started. 'I do not believe, Holmes, that I have ever expressed such an interest to you?'

'My dear fellow, have I not been regularly treated to snatches of music-hall songs which have emanated from your room during your washing and shaving activities?'

I believe I might have blushed. 'I had not intended my singing to be loud enough, during ablutions, even for your sharp ears. In any case, could I not have heard those songs rendered by errand-boys or played upon barrel-organs?'

He considered. 'A fair enough point, though I doubt that

you would have heard, for example, complete verse and chorus of *The Boy in the Gallery* from a passing youth on a cycle. Errand-boys are more inclined to whistle, and street pianos do not have the facility to reproduce the human voice. Oh, and don't tell me that you have heard these compositions played upon Edison's phonograph. Heaven be praised we do not own such a contraption, and neither do any of our immediate neighbours!'

'I must confess,' I muttered, 'I once used to enjoy an evening at Murphy's House on the Green. But that was years ago; why it probably no longer exists!'

'It not only still exists, my dear Watson, but I have booked for us two front stalls for the later performance this very night. Second house is, I believe, the popular term for it. If this does not appeal to you, I will give the tickets to Billy; he could take the girl from the flower shop.'

I tried not to respond too hastily. 'Why no, Holmes, I would be happy to go, and I think you would enjoy it too, despite the light nature of its performances. If you have booked early we may find ourselves seated at the chairman's table.'

'I think not, Watson. You will find that the times are changing and most music halls are now becoming theatres of variety, with seating more like that in a legitimate theatre.'

I suddenly remembered that I had never mentioned the name of the theatre that I could recall. 'The choruses that I warbled could have given you no indication that it was Murphy's that I once frequented.'

'Oh, come, Watson, you have kept programmes and postcard pictures of performers, and these souvenirs have not always been well enough hidden to escape my gimlet gaze.'

It was settled then, and at half past seven of the clock I found myself in a hansom alongside my friend, preparing to recapture the pleasure of a night at the music hall, or as Holmes insisted, 'the Varieties.'

Murphy's theatre was still there on the green as I remembered it, but as Holmes had said, it was now called 'The Varieties', which words were displayed above its façade and spelled out with enough electric bulbs to delight the Swann company. As the patrons from the first house poured out onto the green, my mind took me back to those times in the eighties when last I had frequented Murphy's and the entrance had been lit still with gas jets and the hokey-pokey men had plied their wares with their cry, 'Hokey-pokey, penny a lump!' and aspiring music-hall stars of the future had danced barefooted before the barrel-organs. There were so many changes, but Murphy's was still standing and was moving toward the great new twentieth century that would so soon be with us. No longer 'Murphy's Music Hall', it was yet with us as 'Murphy's Theatre of Varieties', and I had little doubt that most local inhabitants referred to it still as the 'House on the Green.'

As we passed into the auditorium I noticed a difference in the atmosphere. The smell of tobacco smoke was still there, for you could scarcely have a music-hall or variety-theatre atmosphere without it; but missing was that other mixture of aromas of alcohol, orange peel and disinfectant. Those magical sounds of musicians re-tuning however, combined with the noise and jostling of the crowd, were still there. Yet the patrons were different; more the shopkeeping class than the artisan — and there was a smattering of women in the audience. The ladies were rare at the old Murphy's, save for those of dubious reputation.

Of course, the marked difference was in the absence of the tables around which the patrons used to sit. Now there were serried ranks of red-plush seats, such as one would find in a playhouse. But even more of a shock to me was the character of the performance itself. In the old days the show had been mostly made up of chorus singers and comedians who sang comic songs. Most of these artistes had appeared in character costumes and make-ups, which they would change for each song; and the orchestra had played and the audience had been happy enough to wait a couple of minutes for the artiste to reappear in fresh garb. Now, after the lively overture, the acts followed in rapid succession, and there were no introductions, for there was no chairman.

I remarked upon this to Holmes who handed me a printed brochure, saying, 'I paid a penny for this, Watson. The acts are numbered on the list and the numbers, you may notice, are displayed and changed upon an easel to one side of the stage. Not only does Mr Murphy save a chairman's salary, but he gets extra revenue from the sale of these programmes.'

I remember thinking, 'Trust Holmes to notice these things!'

The first half of the performance commenced with a group of young ladies in costumes similar to those of the can-can dancers of Paris. As the orchestra played from *Orpheus in the Underworld*, they kicked up their legs to display much frilly lace; but it was tastefully done and they were soon gone, giving way to an amusing fellow in a checked jacket and striped trousers. His hair was plastered down flat upon his head with bear's grease and his face was decorated with theatrical cosmetics to emphasise his eyes and the arched black brows above them. The tip of his nose had been dotted with crimson and his lips were painted like those of a duchess, yet he still had a mournful expression. As he made his entrance he ogled at the retreating can-can girls while a painted street scene was dropped behind him.

He spoke rapidly, 'Here I am, here you are, so here we are then. Man came first, woman came after and she's been after him ever since! Beware of the woman, look out for the girl and run like the devil from the widow, she's pepper!'

Holmes's face was a study during this monologue and when the comical fellow burst into a song, each line of which ended with the words 'Whoa . . . backpedal', he hid his head in his expressive hands. But, I confess, I thought that Mr T. E. Dunville was an amusing chap. The comedian was followed by the raising of the painted scene to reveal a full stage, tastefully draped and furnished with a single table of the four-legged kitchen variety. Two acrobats in leotards performed amazing acrobatic feats, over and under the table. I glanced at Holmes's programme which listed them as 'Humpsti, Bumpsti and Rabbit'. The latter, when he joined them, proved to be a clown of the human variety, who caused much laughter with his efforts to duplicate the feats of his companions, finally fetching a custard pie determined to throw it at them, but landing instead upon the table face-down in the custard. Holmes, I noted, had dropped his hands from his face and, chuckling, he gently applauded.

He also seemed to enjoy a gentleman billed as 'Chirgwin — The White-eyed Kaffir'. This performer was a tall man, seeming even taller in a skin-tight black costume. His face had been blackened, save for a diamond-shaped area around his right eye. His appearance was bizarre, yet his offering had more of a sentimental than comical appeal. He played a strange instrument rather like a long, thin cello but with a single string, bridged from the instrument with an inflated pig's bladder. His strange voice harmonised with the thin reedy sound of the instrument as he sang to the effect that, 'his fiddle was his sweetheart'. This was well received and the audience would not let him go, there being shouts of 'Blind Boy' . . . 'Blind Boy'. Obviously they knew him well and he was forced to oblige with the song they demanded. In a voice that was more soprano than high tenor, he sang that despite the fact that 'he was a poor blind boy, his heart was indeed full of joy'. I believe Holmes, as a violinist, enjoyed the playing of the strange instrument.

He said to me, 'It is the tuning of the single E string

which gives it that strange, almost eerie sound, Watson.'

I did not reply, merely grunting as I visualised the possibility of Holmes experimenting with such an instrument back at Baker Street. I could only hope for some diversion to occur which might drive all such thoughts from his ever-inquisitive mind. Before the evening had passed my hopes would be realised. But back to that performance at Murphy's: the first half was brought to an end by a buxom young woman whom I seemed to remember from the old days of music hall. She opened with a bright number, wearing a short dress, the skirt flaring out like a tutu and its upper half having a low-cut, tight bodice. She had fair hair of a tone which could hardly be natural and roguish eyes. Her song was full of *double entendres* and produced sly chuckles, climaxed by hearty applause. Then she made a quick change by means of a shawl and sang in a croaking voice that, 'she was past her prime but willing'. Yes, Miss Marie Lloyd had soon driven Holmes's head back into his hands.

Then, to play in a ditty known as 'Another Little Drink', the conductor spun around to show his face to the audience whilst continuing to conduct. At its conclusion he winked hugely to his friends in the audience and pointed at a notice to one side of the stage which depicted an arrow and the words 'Stalls Bar'.

We took ourselves off to that place, Holmes and I, for, though I was not desperate for refreshment, I wanted to recapture the atmosphere of that watering-hole. It was well patronised by an audience until recently allowed the pleasure of consuming their beverages whilst watching the performance. The gleaming glassware with its spar-kling contents passed around a jolly, happy little crowd of imbibers. Among them stood old Murphy himself, much as I remembered him, with his vast expanse of dress vest and gold watch-chain, oiled cowlick of hair and bulbous nose. His once red sideburns had greyed, but he was still easily recognised by an old patron like myself.

'Mr Murphy, how nice to see you again!'

He looked at me keenly and almost at once recognition was in his eyes. 'Bless my soul, if it ain't one of them young rips from the 'ospital! Watkins, ain't it? I had to sling you out once as I remember.'

Sherlock Holmes stifled a snigger, disguising it as a sort of hybrid cough and snort.

I laughed mirthlessly and said, 'I was young then, sir, and your chorus ladies were very attractive.'

He drained his tankard and said, 'Those were the days, eh? My family have run this old theatre as a music hall for three generations, but the times change and we have to change with them. Variety they wants and variety they gets. It's all these accounts of American vaudeville what has done it, Mr Watkins!'

'Watson, actually . . .'

'Yes, that's right, Watkins . . . well, I had a terrible busi-ness converting this place, taking out the tables, putting in seats and working in an extra performance each night; and we do three on Saturday, you know. You see, it's necessary to take more money because variety needs more varied acts and that costs spondulicks. By the way, who is your friend, another sawbones?'

'Why no, this is Mr Sherlock Holmes, the celebrated detective, don't you know.'

'Sherlock Holmes, eh? Well, I may have had a bit of bother but I'm not in the market . . .'

'In the market for what, Mr Murphy?' Holmes asked, sharply.

'Why, a-hiring of your services, of course! I can handle it.'

I sensed that we had struck a raw nerve without any intent. 'Mr Holmes is not here in a professional capacity,' I said. 'We had not heard of any trouble that you may have had, but simply came here for a night out at the varieties!'

He smiled ruefully, saying, 'My mistake. I suppose celebrated detectives don't go around plying for hire anyway. Come over to my table, gentlemen. Let me get you both a drink and I will tell you all about it.'

We repaired to a table in an alcove of the bar where I consumed a glass of ruby wine and Holmes played with a glass of ale. During the time that we conferred, Murphy managed to consume several tankards of stout and a small brandy.

'Well, gents,' he confessed, 'It's like this here, there are quite a few people putting it about that the House on the Green is haunted.'

I had half expected him to continue unprompted, but it needed Holmes to nudge a continuance. 'Come, sir, that is hardly the end of the world. Most old theatres have a ghost, or rather, they are reputed to.'

'Yes, sir, but they usually just get seen gliding about by

patrons and artistes who have had one too many; they don't actually do anything.'

'This one does do things?' I asked.

'What-ho! He do, young Watkins; like stealing things from the dressing-rooms; and one of the artistes had his boots nailed to the floor and filled with treacle while he was on the stage. When he tried to ready himself to go back to his digs you can imagine what he said.'

Holmes smiled, 'Practical jokes, petty thefts; still hardly the end of the world. Have you actually suffered from it financially?'

'Well, to be honest, in a way I have. You see, the stories about the ghost have got round in the business, so it is small wonder that some of the top liners who used to be pleased enough to do a week here are now thinking twice about it and, in some cases, asking for more money! Last night, just when I was thinking that the whole thing was fizzling out, there was this sudden failure of the 'lectrics, right in the middle of Dunville's act. He was wonderful, for, with the whole place in darkness, there could have been a panic, but he carried on making jokes about it until someone got one of the old flares lit and the trouble was put right. The ghost, or his earthly helper, had pulled all the fuses.'

He paused, emptied his glass and arose, saying, 'Well, gents, like I said, it may all blow over and I certainly don't need to bother Mr Holmes with the matter. Second half is starting, in case you want to see it.'

As we took our seats again some dogs, supervised by a stout Scotsman in a kilt, were balancing upon balls. Mercifully, perhaps, we had missed the greater part of this act, which was followed by a juggler, who did some extremely skilled things with clubs, balls and wooden hoops. But his most amazing feat, to my mind, was when he threw a full wine bottle into the air and, as it descended, mouth downward, managed to impale the aperture with the ferrule of an umbrella, opening this in time to prevent himself getting drenched. I glanced at the programme. He was billed as 'Mons Cinquivelli' and I noticed that Holmes had been watching the feat with interest also.

'He has the most amazing co-ordination, Watson,' he commented, 'and see, he also plays the violin.'

The way in which his hands were displayed in the bright spotlight made it possible for me to appreciate the observation that Holmes had made; indentations on the tips and pads of the left-hand fingers which I had noticed on the digits of the detective himself. Holmes's enthusiasm was the most that he had shown since we had entered the theatre, save for a gleam in his eye when old Murphy had been telling us about the theatre ghost. But he sank back miserably in his seat when the juggler made his exit after performing his final feat, that of juggling a chair, a plate and a crumpled sheet of newspaper. Even I, devoid of equilibristic and balancing knowledge, realised the difficulty in dealing with three such contrasting weights.

Other than Miss Lloyd there was another artiste on the bill to be considered a 'star'. Mr George Robey entered to bright music and presented quite a comical appearance with his flat bowler hat, ecclesiastic jacket and knobbly cane. As he lifted the strange headgear he revealed a comic wig of short, bright-red hair which started up as if he were surprised. He had massive eyebrows, either natural or theatrical, but otherwise he was not as heavily disguised with grease-paint as Mr Dunville had been. He made a gesture of dismissal to the musical director and muttered, 'cease', causing the music to die away. The audience were amused and chuckled quite a bit at these preliminary actions, but Mr Robey rounded on them as if he had meant himself to be taken seriously, and spoke in a voice that was classless. He was no commoner, but neither did he have the clipped tones of high education; he fell somewhere between. 'I mean ter say . . . let there be merriment within reason, by all means, but kindly modulate your merriment with a modicum of reserve . . . I mean ter say!'

Holmes relaxed a little and whispered, 'Mr Robey may describe himself as a comedian, but he is in fact an elocutionist.'

The point was a good one, for one felt sure that Mr Robey could have been effective as a lecturer or a cleric. He pronounced his words lovingly, especially the long ones, and when it came to his comic song he had his own vocal peculiarities. Since his vocal utterances were staccato and intermittent, the orchestra seemed to have to make its tempo suit that of the singer, with intervals for the laughter which each line produced.

Then, quite suddenly, its shock effect the more for its being so totally unexpected, there came a crash which brought the performer and the orchestra to silence and a horrified gasp from the audience, followed by shocked hush. A heavy object had dropped from above, missing the famous comedian by no more than a yard. It appeared to be a sack containing heavy material — heavy indeed, to have given it that speed of descent.

The silence was broken by Robey himself. With great presence of mind he said, 'Ladies and gentlemen, how better for your humble, low comedian to finish his act than by bringing the house down?'

Then he gave a sign to the musical director to cue his musicians in that same bright music with which the act had begun. Robey raised his hat and made a lively exit.

The band played the National Anthem and the audience began to disperse, most of them in lively discourse concerning the events of the few minutes past. As we, also, rose to leave our seats, old Murphy was suddenly at our side. 'Mr Holmes, I was wrong,' he confessed. 'I do need the services of a consulting detective!'

CHAPTER TWO

Backstage at the Varieties

Within two or three minutes we were standing upon the stage of Murphy's theatre of varieties, having forgone the niceties of using the stage door by climbing those steps at the side of the stage itself, normally forbidden to all save performers wishing to make contact with their audience. We surveyed the sandbag — for that it proved to be — that had narrowly missed ending such a promising career as that of Mr George Robey. The comedian himself had returned to the stage to inspect it, as various other performers, now without their motley and in street attire, stood at a respectful distance, some of them casting nervous glances upon that area above from which the missive had come.

Holmes noted that the rope, about eight inches of which was still attached to the bag, had been cleanly cut. He said to the theatre owner, 'Mr Murphy, my knowledge of backstage matters is fairly limited, but I assume that the sandbag is a counterweight involved with the raising and lowering of scenery?'

'That is correct, Mr Holmes. We have had them fall before but, happily, not very often and usually the only cause is the rotting of the rope involved. Naturally, I check them regularly — or rather my head flyman does. Paddy Cox is a reliable man, but in any case I don't need a detective to tell me that the rope was cut with a knife.'

Holmes nodded to signify that he agreed with these words, in substance at least, but clarified, 'With a razor in fact. It was extremely sharp and wielded by a left-handed person. Notice that the direction of the cut is not made in a downward direction, quite the opposite, typical of the left-handed.'

I was a little puzzled, and asked, 'Given this to be correct in your experience, Holmes, how can you tell from which direction the cut commenced?'

Holmes answered, all but pityingly, 'The cut is slanting, and one can see how clean it is where it was commenced, but at the top of the incline there is a certain roughness caused by a combination of the downward pull and the slowing of the velocity of the action of cutting. More than this I can only learn by visiting the original position of the bag; I believe I heard you refer to the area as the flies?'

'It is a bit risky, Mr Holmes, especially if you have no experience of fly work!'

But my friend waved aside Murphy's objections. 'I have some experience of mountain scaling, sir. In fact, Watson will tell you that I once fell several hundred feet at the Reichenbach Falls and lived to tell the tale!'

'Or so it was believed,' I muttered.

Murphy shrugged and said, 'On your head be it, sir, or is

that an unfortunate phrase? Well, follow me and I'll point you in the direction you must take. You will forgive me if I do not accompany you but I have no head for heights myself and would suggest that young Wilkins stays upon terra-cotta, because I have noticed that he has a game leg.'

Having given me yet another surname and illustrated his ability to create malapropisms, Murphy introduced us to the head flyman, Paddy Cox. That worthy cast an eye over Holmes's lean frame and nodded, 'You can make it easy enough, guv'nor, but I'm not taking the others up there; more than my position and reputation is worth should one of 'em come a buster!'

I assumed that 'come a buster' was backstage argot for falling to one's death, or sustaining serious injury at the very least. I nodded my approval, deciding to allow Holmes his desire to be the lone hero.

As my daring friend ascended the ladder at the side of the stage, I glanced around me in the hope that I might notice something that would lend some clue to the extraordinary events of the evening. I soon found that I could add little to that which Holmes had discovered, so I turned my energies to questioning one or two of the assembled artistes. Murphy told me that he had decided not to inform the police about the possibility of a serious attempt upon the life of one of his artistes.

'Less said about this, the better, young Watling. I just want your friend to find out what's behind all this business so that I can deal with it myself. It's not good for the patrons to hear what they don't need to, and it's already getting difficult to get artistes to work here, as I told you.'

He touched his nose with the tip of his right index finger in a most conspiratorial manner as he spoke these words.

'It is up to you, of course,' I said, 'for there is no definite proof, as yet, that the whole thing is more than an accident. But you know, my dear Murphy, the longer you put off taking definite action regarding a problem, the harder it is when you have to do so. If this sort of thing continues, your hand will be forced. Suppose Mr Robey had been killed — or even just injured. The publicity would, indeed, have been detrimental to your business. Who knows what might happen next?'

He nodded glumly and I added, 'From what you have told me the mishaps began in a very small way and gradually increased in their seriousness. But this first near-tragedy may not be the last, or worst, of such episodes.'

The hour was now quite late and the artistes who had still been present at the time of the accident were restless to leave. No one had insisted that they stay, but the serious nature of the accident had nudged the cameraderie of their profession.

Old Murphy, however, gave them that permission which both he and they knew to be unnecessary. 'Thanks for staying, boys and girls. Not much we can do tonight, unless Mr Holmes wishes to ask you any questions?'

Holmes shook his head, a little to my surprise, saying quietly to me, 'Those from whom we could learn anything have probably already left the building.' Then he raised his voice to speak to the theatre owner, 'I feel that Watson and I should take this opportunity to return to Baker Street, but I will return tomorrow when I have had a chance to consider that which has transpired. I have no doubt that Mr Robey wishes to change from his motley and return home also.'

Robey nodded his gratitude and walked off in the direction of his dressing-room. Murphy grunted, 'Never hired a detective before, but I don't seem to be getting much for my money as yet. Always the same. Take old Robey; charges me a little more for every week's engagement that I give him. Whenever I mention it, he buys me a glass of stout in the bar. I give him guineas, and he gives me Guinness.'

We chuckled politely at his pun and walked briskly towards the front lobby of the theatre. I was anxious to hear what discoveries might have been made by Holmes in the flies. He was silent in the cab in which we returned and not particularly communicative as we sat by the fire having a final pipe. I spoke temptingly, to try and bring Holmes from his reverie. 'Robey took it all pretty calmly, I thought.'

He relit his pipe with a hot cinder held in the fire-tongs. His answering grunt was hardly encouraging.

I tried again, 'A strange turn of events, as whoever, or whatever, is responsible, for I suppose we cannot entirely discount psychic agency, has suddenly made a big jump from that which would appear to be a series of practical jokes to a far more serious action.'

Another grunt of a reply made me lose all patience and ask a question which demanded an answer, 'Holmes, did you discover anything of moment up in the theatre flies?'

Even so, Holmes was slow to reply, making sure that his pipe was burning to his satisfaction before he spoke.

But when he did, he spoke to me with an unexpected patience. 'My dear Watson, forgive my seemingly rude dismissiveness, but my mind has been taking me down a number of paths, none of which would appear to lead it to its goal. In answer to your several questions: yes, George Robey seems to be quite a solid man, not easily frightened; and yes, I do agree that the events have taken a brisk turn from the trivial to the near-tragic. As to your third question, the only one which appeared to need a genuine answer, I did not discover anything which I expected or half-hoped for. The flymen had seen nothing and I found no blade or tell-tale signs that might have helped me. However, I am not unobservant, as you have long noticed if your scribblings are accurate of your real feelings. To begin with, the boards upon which the flymen tread in order to do their work have been replaced in fairly recent times; yet some of them, only some, are bowed as if a heavily-built person had spent some time upon them. All the flymen are of light build, a qualification for their trade. Moreover, as I have hinted, only boards in certain places are thus misshaped. George Robey is the first person to have suffered more than minor irritation through the antics of the so-called ghost. Yes, you are right not to discount a psychic connection. We may not believe in such things but should not discount anything. I believe we should pay a visit to Mr Robey at his home in the morning. Eleven of the clock, Watson, should you be awake by then to accompany me.'

I took his sarcasm in good part and decided to turn in. As I arose with this in mind, Holmes said, 'Sleep well, Watson. Oh, and whilst you are on your feet, could you be so kind as to pass me the album with the green cloth cover?'

*

'Ah, Watson, at last you have arisen from your sleep of the good and just. Perhaps some day, if I change my style of living, I too will be able to enjoy a long, blameless slumber. It is past nine by several minutes and I have already sent a telegram to Robey.'

I was a little puzzled, 'It occurred to me, before sleep blurred my mind, that you had not taken Robey's card. How did you obtain his address?'

'Watson, I am resourceful. I knew that within that album which you passed to me on your way to your appointment with Morpheus, there reposed a recently purchased copy of a theatrical journal, in which I remembered that all the leading vaudeville lights advertise their presence. Robey was listed, as I knew he would be.'

'Has he replied yet?'

As if in answer to my question there was a tap upon the door and Billy entered with a wire.

Holmes chuckled. 'Watson, if you had witnessed this little scene in a play at the Lyceum, you would have accused the playwright of being rather obvious. However, this is real life, not drama, and in real life there are no golden rules for events to follow.'

He picked up a clean butter-knife from the breakfast table and deftly slit the flap of the envelope. He scanned the telegram quickly. 'Billy, you may fetch a hansom for the doctor and myself. Quickly now, but not so very quickly that I might suspect you of fetching the first cab you come upon!'

Billy reddened as he ran off and I enquired of Holmes, 'Did you really suspect the boy of such carelessness?'

'Not at all. I know Billy well . . . his blush was of anger that I should think it of him. He never blushes when accused of actual wrongdoing.'

As Holmes removed his robe I realised that he was already wearing formal morning trousers and waistcoat. He had only to slip into his black frock-coat and pick up his top hat from the peg. I was already formally dressed so we lost a minimum of time.

As we climbed into the hansom the driver leaned over and said, 'What ho, Mr Holmes! You want to buck that boy of yours up a bit. Do you know there were two vacant cabs immediately in front of me and he let them pass by as if he was in a trance.'

George Robey greeted us heartily and, even without his makeup and motley, he was very easily recognisable. As he stood at his garden gate, watching out for us, an errand-boy on a bicycle passed and yelled, 'Wotcha, George'. Robey waved and smiled good-naturedly. He shook hands with us warmly and ushered us into his pleasant villa which seemed to be furnished with mementoes rather than the more usual objects. There were framed portraits everywhere of Mr Robey in various character guises, from prehistoric men to brides! Each ornament had to be lovingly lifted and shown to us, a story to go with each. However, he sensed that Holmes wished serious discussion and suggested, 'I have a quiet retreat in the garden, gentlemen. I propose we go there where we will not be disturbed by wives or domestics.'

I admired the actor's full mouth that he gave to every word.

'It is a workshop you take us to?' Holmes enquired.

'How did you know that?'

'I didn't, but suspected as much from the varnish upon your fingernails. You are a carpenter, Mr Robey?'

He was mildly surprised at the near accuracy Holmes displayed, and expounded, 'Nearly; in fact my hobby is the construction of violins.'

Holmes nodded, 'You make them, yet you do not play them.'

'How can you tell?'

'From your fingers. The tips and pads of neither hand display those tell-tale indentations which your juggling colleague enjoys.'

He raised his famous eyebrows, 'Upon my word, I salute your observation, sir. Yes, young Cinquivelli plays but does not make, I make but do not play. Strange, I suppose, but I am fascinated with the construction of that most elegant and soulful of all musical instruments. Are you a violinist, sir?'

As if in answer, Holmes held out his hands, palms up, that Robey might see the indentations on the fingers of his left hand. 'I would not describe myself as a violinist, but I do play, for my own entertainment and to the annoyance of those about me. I am fortunate enough to own a Stradivarius.'

The comedian threw up his hands in wonder. 'Upon my word, you must be a millionaire. I had no idea that crime detection was so profitable. I can see that I am in the wrong business.'

Holmes chuckled, but did not relate the story of his ownership of the almost priceless instrument.

Then as Robey unlocked the door of the compact

outbuilding, which he had referred to as his workshop, it was our turn to throw up our hands in wonder and awe. It was quite the neatest and most tasteful workshop that I had ever seen. There were carpenter's bench and lathe, together with a few compact tools, all practically free of wood-dust or shavings, to one side. On the other side was a table upon which rested Robey's current project, or so it appeared. At the far end there was a glass case in which there rested half a dozen beautiful instruments. Robey rubbed his hands with a proprietorial air. 'All me own work, gents, as a pavement artist would say!'

Each instrument was, or appeared to be, quite perfect; yet one of them, centrally positioned, caught the eye the most.

He gestured towards it, 'I call that my Gelado!'

Holmes inspected it with interest. 'My dear Robey, I would defy anyone to know this from an instrument made by the great Gelado, a name which afficionados revere, even more than that of Stradivarius himself. Do you think I might have the honour of playing a bar or two upon it?'

Robey promptly opened the case, took out the instrument and handed it to Holmes, along with a bow. My friend deftly tuned the violin, put it up to his left shoulder and drew the bow across it experimentally. There followed a few bars of *Liebestraum* which even my rough-hewn musical ear told me was the most perfect tone possible.

Robey was ecstatic. 'Upon my word, you are such a player, sir. I cannot believe that I have created an instrument which not only appears just like a Gelado but sounds just like it too. I have never heard it played before.'

Holmes was almost apologetic in his tone as he answered, 'The reason that you fancy it sounds just like a Gelado is because it actually *is* such an instrument.'

Robey rounded on him with mock horror. 'Nonsense, sir, you jest! I made that violin myself; it took me a year studying illustrations and, finally, an actual example in the Museum of Stringed Masterpieces in Croydon. Please explain your remark, sir!'

I admit that I, too, wondered if Holmes could be jesting in the worst of taste, yet could read from his expression that he was in deadly earnest. 'The wonderful tone is unmistakable and the maker's label inside is authentic.'

'Such things can be forged . . . ,' I ventured.

Robey backed this up. 'I have a friend who imitates these little finishing touches for me. I asked him to look at the label in the example in the museum and you can see the result.'

Holmes shook his head. 'That particular manner in which the paper has been fixed cannot be imitated, at least not successfully. This instrument is a genuine Gelado.'

Robey gave the picture of a man in a dream. Eventually his astonishment led to a flood of vocal expression. 'What can this mean . . . it looks identical to the one I made . . . how did it get here and where on earth is my facsimile?'

'I do not, as yet, know the answers to your questions, my dear Robey, nor that to my own, which is why would anyone do this? For someone has brought the situation about, it is no mystical happening.'

I broke in with what I thought to be a pertinent point. 'Surely, somewhere, someone is missing a Gelado, unless

Mr Robey has a secret millionaire benefactor?'

George Robey proved, despite his calling, to be a man of obvious taste and refinement, for not only had he built a Gelado, but he served us with Turkish coffee in authentic tiny cups. As we sipped the scalding ink-black liquid, I made to light my pipe, noting that Robey was smoking a cigarette, but Holmes waved an admonishing hand at me. 'My dear Watson, one does not produce tobacco smoke near an authentic Gelado. It will darken the wood!'

I put away my briar as Robey ground his cigarette on the ashtray, admonished in his own workshop.

I muttered what I believed to be a fair comment. 'Your Strad gets no such care, Holmes.'

There was a glint in my friend's eye as he answered me, 'All hope for the well-being of my Stradivarius was lost years ago, Watson. I regard it not as a collector's piece, status symbol or tool of my trade; therefore I can ill-treat it to my heart's content, and I do, but its tone is still pure.'

Robey looked a little uncertain before he spoke again. 'Mr Holmes, will you give me the benefit of your professional attention in this case of the materialising Gelado?'

My friend considered thoughtfully before he replied. 'I am intrigued enough to answer in the affirmative, but you must understand that I am presently engaged in the matter of Murphy's ghostly happenings at his House on the Green. I must try to make some progress in that matter first; meanwhile, my advice to you, sir, is to remove the Gelado from this insecure workshop and guard it with your life.'

'The workshop is, I am assured by experts, extremely secure!'

'How then did an intruder transpose the instruments?'

Robey nodded wisely, 'I take your point, Holmes. I will keep it in my safe.'

'That is wise, and I further suggest that you mention this matter to no one.'

George Robey was an extremely successful man in a business in which one can, I have been told, be very much up or down. This was an up I decided, when he offered to send us to Murphy's Variety Theatre in his motor car, one of but a handful in the north of London at that time. Looking back it was, I believe, one of the very first occasions on which I travelled in such an equipage. As we sped past terrified horses and pedestrians, we realised that we could not discuss the matter of the phantom Gelado within earshot of the driver. For privacy give me a hansom any time.

Old Murphy was standing in the lobby of the theatre as if expecting us. He took us to his office, an extension of the box-office, containing safes and pigeon holes for papers. Here Holmes felt free to smoke, whispering to me, 'Money improves with use and signs of wear and tear.'

Although we could not confide in Murphy concerning the mystery of the Gelado violin, Holmes did ask a few questions concerning George Robey. They were not of an impertinent nature but hardly enquiries one would make of the gentleman himself. Holmes craftily wove such questions in amongst those concerning other artistes on the bill at the Varieties. 'Your top of the bill is quite a young man to have gained such fame?'

'George is a little short of thirty; he has a long career ahead of him and I reckon he will go as high as is possible. Already he is thinking of calling himself "The Prime Minister of Mirth". He's a good draw, and also a good businessman; strikes a hard bargain, does George. I've employed him many times, but always for a little more money. But this may be the last week he plays here, for I'll wager he'll want even more next time, and the house won't stand it. Can't put the price of the seats up the way things are at the moment. D'ye hear anything?'

We both said that we could hear nothing unusual; just the street sounds from without and the sounds made by cleaners and artisans within. Murphy nodded, 'Exactly, and that is strange, because the room next to this is a spare one where I have let Duncan keep his collies for the week. They are usually barking their heads off by midday when they know he will arrive to let them out. He is late too, so it's even more surprising.'

We discussed the other artistes on the bill, all of whom seemed to be above descending to practical jokes or, even more so, to dangerous acts like the dropping of a sandbag. Moreover, these artistes were at the theatre for that week only, and the minor incidents had been happening for quite a while.

'Other than the artistes, there are your regular staff. I assume you trust them all?'

'Been with me years, Mr Holmes, since before we became the Varieties. Most of them go back to the old oncenightly music-hall days.'

A thought occurred to me. 'How about regular patrons?

Are any of them to be suspected in any way? I mean, known criminal types or anything like that?'

'None that I have upset, or could wish me any harm. I get on well with all my regulars, for it takes all kinds to make a world, does it not?'

However, Holmes took up my point. 'Were none of them upset by your change of policy, from music hall to variety?'

'Oh well, a few of the old diehards grumbled and, of course, old Shelby, the chairman, was not exactly delighted to lose his job, but still comes to almost every performance from force of habit. Naturally, I let him in on his Wilkie . . . not that he ever needs to show it.'

I was puzzled. 'His . . . his Wilkie?'

But it was Holmes rather than Murphy who explained. 'I have been burning the midnight oil recently, Watson, regarding the music hall and variety theatres; Wilkie Bard is a famous music-hall comic singer, and bard rhymes with card, does it not?'

'I still don't quite understand . . .'

'Upon my word, Watson, I can't make it much clearer. It is a custom in the profession for a known artiste to be admitted free of charge on showing his card to the manager. Cockney rhyming slang has turned card to Wilkie Bard, and shortened it to Wilkie.'

'Why do they not just say "card"?'

'You are a killjoy, Watson. That would spoil everything!'

This minor argument was interrupted by the rotund Mr Duncan, no longer in his tartan but still sounding very Scottish. He nodded to Murphy as he placed a key in the lock of the spare apartment from which joyful barks and yelps should have been emanating. The poor man's face was a study as he threw open the door to reveal a room empty, save for a number of dog baskets and water bowls.

He rounded on Murphy, 'What have you done wi' ma buffers?'

I tried to work out in my mind a word that would both rhyme with buffer and connect in some way with canines but without success. Murphy replied sharply, 'I have no idea; you locked them up last night, that's all I know!'

Duncan ran out of the room, alternately shouting and whistling, 'Bess! Rex! Charlie! Where are ye?'

To his great joy his voice was answered by a series of barks, yaps and yelps, seemingly from the direction of the backstage area. He made for these sounds and we followed. His ear took him to his dressing-room where he fairly tore the door open to be greeted by such a bounding and jumping. It was a joyful reunion of man and dogs. The several animals were checked by Duncan, who announced that they were all quite healthy.

Murphy voiced the general opinion, 'Someone must have brought them up here during the night, but who, and why?'

Holmes remarked, by way of answer, 'The same being, actual or ethereal, who dropped the sandbag, turned off the lighting and decided to return to less harmful pranks; at least, for the time being.'

'Fetch Harrison!' Murphy was shouting, it transpired, for his nightwatchman to be brought to him. A minion was dispatched to rouse the by-now-sleeping watchman from his bed in his nearby home. He later appeared, un-shaven and grumbling drowsily. Murphy presented him with the riddle of the transferred canines, and the watchman scratched his stubbly, grey head. 'Whoever moved them dogs without my seeing or hearing must have known what they were about. If a stranger had tried it they would have barked their heads off. I think you are looking for the work of Tom Elcott here. Those dogs were not led up to that dressing-room, they were transported there supernaturally.'

Holmes grunted and said, 'I assume you are referring to the famous theatre ghost. This is the first time he has been given a name in my hearing. So the ghost is one Tom Elcott? Did he appear at this theatre?'

Murphy tried to dismiss this aspect, 'That old chestnut! There was a comic singer, Tom Elcott, who appeared here some thirty years ago. He was not a success and he took it very badly and hung himself in dressing-room five.'

I remarked, 'It sounds as if he took his lack of success very badly indeed. Do many music-hall performers take their own lives?'

Murphy said, 'Not many. If they are not a success for any length of time, they more often take to drink or leave the profession altogether. I think I can say that Elcott was the only suicide we have ever had at the House on the Green.'

Harrison leapt in. 'What about Mary Malone? Back when I was stage manager, she died from an overdose of laudanum or some such. Then, there was Jimmy Grant, "The Whistling Drummer-boy" who threw himself down the dressing-room stairwell.'

Again Murphy was obviously unwilling to allow the conversation to continue to follow the path it was taking.

'Better get back to your Uncle Ned, Albert, or you'll be good for nothing tonight.'

Then, as the grumbling watchman shuffled off, Murphy turned to us. 'Take no notice of Albert Harrison, he's been here for years and has never got over being taken away from his backstage job and put to being watchman. Mary Malone was no better than she should have been and it was never proved that she meant to do herself in. As for Jimmy Grant, I always thought that he fell, rather than deliberately went, down the stairwell.'

Then the bibulous theatre owner led us to the stalls bar, which, we learned, was open for business at times other than during performances. Murphy seemed more at home in its cosy atmosphere than in his office. One or two other regular disciples of Bacchus were already seated upon bar stools and around tables. Shelby, the former chairman, who I remembered well from my days of regular patronage, was in jovial mood. He lifted his tankard and declared for the benefit of the half-dozen regulars, 'Ladies and gentlemen, we bring you, at no doubt enormous expense, that famous enquirer into misdeeds, that scourge of the criminal classes, that fly in the frauds ointment and persecutor of pilferers, your own, if you don't watch out, Mr Sherlock Holmes.'

There was a little sniggering but my friend took it in good part. He studied Shelby carefully before he replied, 'It is hardly my intention to be in any of those categories, Mr Chairman, if I may still use your former title, but it is hardly fair that I should receive such a splendid introduction without returning the compliment.'

'You mean you could do my job as well as your own?'

Holmes adopted an expansive air as he addressed the assembled few listeners. 'Ladies and gentlemen, may I introduce a man who is a martyr to liver problems, and keeps a bull terrier; a widower who spends at least one evening a week in all male company, but with a female involvement, and who has recently consulted a fortune-teller . . .'

Shelby sprang to his feet, red-faced and shaking, 'Oh! So you've been sticking your nose into my business and for quite some time, eh, Mr Busybody?'

Holmes placated him. 'My dear Mr Shelby, I met you last evening for the very first time and have been far too busy since to give any interest to your affairs. But to the trained eye a great deal which would escape that of the casual observer is plain to see. For example, let me begin with that which is most obvious, your ownership of a bull terrier. The short, stiff hairs upon the sleeves of your jacket tell their own story. You wear a wedding ring, yet the jacket is not regularly brushed; this points to your being a widower.'

Shelby started, and then calmed. 'Oh, I see, simple when you know how, as Carlton, the conjurer, says. But how do you know that I am troubled with my liver?'

'The small veins upon your nose, and the flush of your complexion betray your fondness for the company of John Barleycorn, which is inevitably followed by problems with the liver, as I think Dr Watson will testify?'

I was forced to concur. 'That is indeed so. I have no doubt that your own doctor has warned you in this direction, Mr Shelby?'

The former chairman grunted. 'He is a quack and a

charlatan, I have no need of his advice. But, Holmes, you can't get away that easily; how do you know that I spend one evening a week in all-male company?'

Holmes admitted, 'It could be less often, but certainly a man who wears Masonic jewellery would attend frequent meetings to which women would not be admitted.'

Shelby nodded. 'I can see that there is a certain skill in your calling, but admit now that a certain amount of guess-work is involved. There are times, are there not, when you either hit or miss? For example, my visit to a fortune-teller; what hint could you possibly have had concerning that?'

Holmes conceded, 'I noticed the palmist's premises near the theatre but thought little of this until I noticed that your right palm has been recently cleansed. This morning you left home in a hurry, not stopping even to wash; but then, on a whim, you decided to visit the palmist and attempted to clean your palm by means of saliva and your display handkerchief.'

The detective neatly turned the white linen square which projected from Shelby's breast pocket so that its soiled opposite portion could be seen. Shelby hastily rearranged the handkerchief to some state of respectability.

He had reddened as much as his already flushed face would allow. 'Very well, Mr Clever Dick, but you have one thing left to explain. Where do you get the idea of a female involvement in my life?'

'Oh, come, my dear Shelby! What else would cause a man of your years to visit a palmist save an *affaire de coeur*? To the trained eye all the pieces of a puzzle can be fitted together.'

Shelby was at first angry, but then began to chuckle. 'Upon my word, Holmes, you are shrewd indeed, and I pity the poor old ghost once you get onto his trail!'

Holmes became more intense in his manner. 'You believe then that a ghost is responsible for some of the occurrences which have troubled this theatre, Shelby?'

The ex-chairman narrowed his eyes as he spoke, 'That I cannot say for sure, but of one thing I am certain, there *is* a ghost, malevolent or no!'

'You have seen it yourself?'

'Aye, often enough through the years, and I regarded it as a rather benevolent spirit. But its attitude has recently changed and I think it is possible that *it* is *he* who dropped the sandbag and nearly finished Robey's career; and surely a ghostly hand darkened the theatre. He started with pranks, but his actions have become gradually more dangerous. You want to hear old Charters on the subject!'

Shelby pointed to one of his cronies who appeared to try to lose himself in his greatcoat and showed great interest in his beer and his pipe, but Holmes has always had a charm of manner which he can unexpectedly bring to the fore. 'Mr Charters, I fancy I am right in saying that you have been a regular patron of the House on the Green for many years. I deduce this from the vesta case which lies before you on the table. It bears a likeness of Miss Bessie Bellwood, a soubrette of a long-passed era. You are a supporter of the music hall and your views upon the subject under discussion would be valuable, nay invaluable, I feel sure.'

Charters's head emerged from the collar of his coat like a tortoise peering out of its shell, but there the reptilian likeness ceased, for he had a bright eye when thus cajoled.

He spoke in a rather shaky voice, not unusual in a man of his, perhaps, seventy years. 'Yes, sir, I have been coming to this theatre for a great many years and I could tell you much about the great old days of music hall. Now they are trying to make it respectable and they call it "variety". Well, that is well and good, but where will it stop? Already they have taken away the chairman, the tables and the beer. But at least we are still allowed to smoke.'

I felt I had a contribution to make to the conversation. 'But surely, Mr Charters, this new variety theatre still includes some stars of the music hall?'

'Correct, sir, but more and more of the turns would have been considered more suitable for a circus in the old days, and we miss the chairman. Still, it's all to do with pounds, shillings and pence these days. They can get in the two houses now, and three on Saturdays. Why, the show used to last for three hours at least, and it would allow for a leisurely pace with the chairman making comical remarks between the turns, and introducing well-known people in the audience and so on. You could have a real good night out for a couple of bob.'

Holmes was impatient to lead Charters into the direction which he wished him to do. 'Concerning the ghost, you have yourself encountered it?'

'Yes, once I met him, standing in the shadows near the left-hand stalls' exit. I had returned to get my hat which I had left behind when leaving the theatre. When I slipped back it happened there was no one else about, and his sudden appearance gave me quite a turn. He was in leotards, like an acrobat, and he seemed to disappear as quickly as he must have arrived.'

'You mean he faded away?'

'Not quite. You see, I looked around to see if there was anyone else about to confirm what I could see. When I looked back, he just was not there anymore.'

'You say he was in leotards; had any of the artistes in the performance you had attended been thus attired?'

'No, Mr Holmes, there were no acrobats that week, and anyway . . .' He paused, as if he might not wish to say more.

Holmes, however, managed to persuade him to restart his narrative. 'Come, Mr Charters, you are among friends, and I will not mock anything you may say. After all, you are evidently not alone in these sightings of the seemingly supernatural.'

Hesitatingly, Charters continued, 'I was about to say that there was, in any case, something a trifle — what is the word — ethereal about him. He was deathly pale of complexion and wore white tights, which added to the ghostliness of his appearance.'

'You say there were other occasions when you sighted this seeming spectre?'

'Perhaps the most memorable was when I was alone in the theatre very late at night, in my official capacity.'

'You are a carpenter, are you not?'

'Why, yes, sir. Do my hands betray my trade?'

'No, it is your manner of breathing. I have long noticed that a professional carpenter expels his breath as if to repel flying sawdust. The intake of the breath is interesting too, through all but closed lips, also to avoid shavings in the mouth. But please continue with your story.'

'I was working on a moulding on the side proscenium arch when I sensed that something was happening in the flies. I walked to centre-stage and looked up to see a ghostly figure — remember I had only a lamp to work by — in white, swinging like a pendulum from a rope.'

'How far up?'

'Oh, about forty to fifty feet. The theatre dome is immediately above the stage and as far as I could make out the figure was swinging close to the inside of the dome itself.'

'Did it fade away, or disappear, as in the other account you gave us?'

'Neither, sir. He swung up onto the walkway where the flymen work. But, of course, they had all left hours earlier.'

At this point Holmes insisted on buying a drink for the assembled patrons. This widened the scope of the ghost stories to include the improbable, unlikely and downright impossible. But at least the acrobat in the white leotards was consistent. One worthy even insisted that the ghost had followed him out of the theatre and sat with him on the top of a horse-bus.

The raconteur continued, 'I wouldn't have minded, only he had no money with him and I had to pay his fare!'

Such comments we endured in order to learn what we could from those made by more responsible persons.

CHAPTER THREE

Fiddlers' Paradise

It was in the afternoon of that same day that we arrived at Croydon where the curator of the Museum of Stringed Masterpieces was expecting us. That worthy, one Professor Septimus Crockett, proved to be an earnest, elderly man of obvious learning and culture. He had that stoop, popularly referred to as 'scholarly', but which probably had a medical rather than scholastic history. He led us through rooms lined with glass cases where the serried ranks of violins, cellos and harps presented a monotony not usually coupled with the pleasure that these instruments could bring. Mercifully, the room was eventually reached where the celebrated Gelado was housed. Crockett threw back his mane of shoulder-length, silver hair and indicated the principal show case.

'There it is, gentlemen, the jewel in our crown, so to speak, the pride of our collection. As you can see, it is still safely housed in a secure show case, firmly locked, and whilst your concern is appreciated, it is hardly justified.'

'You have not, then, examined the instrument since you received my message?'

The cadence of Holmes's voice made his question rather more like a statement.

'How do you know that, sir?'

'Because, Professor, if you had, you would be wringing your hands in horror rather than proudly indicating the facsimile which now rests in the case.'

'I think you will find that it is our Gelado; the case is undisturbed and I would soon spot any change in an instrument which I have proudly observed for so many years.'

Holmes shrugged. 'The lock has been recently opened, either with a bent wire, or even with a teaspoon handle!'

The professor was losing patience. 'What nonsense, sir. That lock cost us a great deal of money. It could certainly not be opened with a teaspoon!'

My friend took his lens from his pocket and examined the lock closely. Then he spoke apologetically, 'My mistake, Professor, it was neither a teaspoon nor yet a wire pick. The lock was sprung with a corkscrew. But, just to prove my point, I will open it for you with an even simpler implement.'

Holmes took out his several-bladed pocket-knife and, using one of its attachments, was as good as his word in opening the lock.

'This particular blade is really intended for the removal of stones from the hooves of quadrupeds. I have never had occasion to use it for its correct purpose, but I have often used it as a means of laying open to me that which was secured.'

The professor, doubt in his eyes for the first time, swung

the door of the case open and grasped the instrument, bringing it forth gently despite his impatient concern.

But he evidently found a perfunctory examination reassuring. 'My dear sir, you have wasted my time; just look at that workmanship. Why, no modern craftsman could so closely imitate the work of the master!'

Holmes nodded, as if expecting the outburst. 'There is one modern craftsman who could, and has, imitated it so superbly. Please look carefully at the maker's label, and use my lens if you wish.'

But Crockett needed no lens to appreciate that the label was not genuine. Moreover, he soon ascertained that a minor defect in the neck of the instrument was no longer there. He was like a broken man and full of contrition.

'My dear Holmes, my apologies. You are, of course, right; this is not our Gelado, just a brilliant copy. See how the maker has imitated the aged varnish! Do you suspect the identity of this genius?'

My friend chuckled, 'Would it surprise you to learn that it was made by a music-hall comedian who builds violins in his garden workshop?'

Crockett was beginning to succumb to the strain of the happening. 'You mock me, sir, and it is unworthy of you! I not only feel bereaved by the loss of the Gelado, but my career as museum curator will be over. Only a master craftsman could have made this.'

'You consider then that a comedian could not also be a master craftsman, building wonderful musical instruments as a hobby? I am, however, more interested at present in identifying the person who purloined the original. Have you noticed anyone who might have shown more than a casual interest in the Gelado recently?'

The curator's apologetic air resumed. 'Not of late, but I can remember a rather stockily-built man with pronounced eyebrows making frequent visits a year or so ago, and always stopping in front of the Gelado, sometimes for quite protracted periods. Do you think he was the thief?'

'No, sir, I believe he was the craftsman who made the instrument you hold. I have no reason to suspect that he made the copy with any kind of ulterior motive.'

Crockett returned the instrument to its case, which he relocked upon Holmes's instruction.

He was a spent force and, as he gave us tea in his office, assumed a hangdog manner. 'What am I to do? I would give all that I own for the return of the Gelado, but I imagine that would scarcely suffice. Whoever has our violin must be expecting to get a fortune for it.'

Holmes calmed him. 'Professor Crockett, you will not, I believe, need to part with any of your savings or chattels. I think I can promise the return of your Gelado within a few days. All I ask of you in return is that you do not make the substitution known to anyone else.'

The promise was not difficult to obtain and we left Professor Crockett in a somewhat more sanguine mood. I was a little puzzled as to why Holmes had appealed for secrecy, especially as he well knew where the famous Gelado rested. I remarked to this effect as we returned to Baker Street in a hansom. Holmes did not fully enlighten me. 'Watson, things are best left as they are for the moment.

The culprit who exchanged the instruments cannot get the Gelado from Robey's safe; and I would rather that he remained in ignorance of our own limited knowledge of the affair.'

'But why did he do it, Holmes? If he was so easily able to steal the Gelado from the museum, why did he not simply keep it for whatever purpose he stole it?'

'If I knew that, all would be far simpler, Watson. Obviously he plays some sort of waiting game, and the longer he believes that his actions are not suspected the better, and the greater our chance to observe when he does make some kind of move.'

We spent another evening at the Varieties, quietly observing. The stalls bar was all but empty during the opening half of the first of the two performances and we were able to sit in a corner and discuss it all in comparative secrecy. We had learned from the barmaid that the ghost had made yet another appearance; this time appearing to her in the bar itself where, arriving early, she had seen it, momentarily, standing behind the bar. She had insisted that the visitant was Mary Malone.

Holmes raised an aspect of the affair to which I had not thus far given thought. 'Watson, you do realise that we are dealing with more than one ghost, if such it is that has been seen. We have heard some accounts of a female ghost, and a male acrobat in leotards, still capable of performing his acrobatic skills, as well as standing glowering in shadows.'

My response was a bewildered one.

'Well, Holmes, I suppose the same ghost could appear in

various earthly forms. Who knows what a ghost might be able to do?'

Sherlock Holmes threw back his head and would have laughed loudly, I feel sure, had we not been in a public place, be it so secluded.

'Oh Watson, you are priceless! You speak so seriously about ghosts and their various abilities as if such things were beyond all doubt. I may say that one should discount nothing, but all my thoughts and energies are being thrown into the search for human agencies, singular or plural.'

'You mean we should be looking for perhaps two persons who are playing at ghosts?'

'Such thoughts had crossed my mind, my dear fellow, but if you think we should be engaging the services of a spirit medium or a cleric specialising in the dismissal of troublesome spirits then please do not let me stand in your way!'

'You mean an exorcist?'

'The word had eluded me, Watson, but I'm sure you have the right one. However, whilst keeping an open mind, I feel that we should continue to investigate the probability of some persons who for reasons best known to themselves have decided to play ghost.'

I responded as constructively as I could. 'You know, students often play pranks. Could it be a series of japes from such a quarter?'

'Japes, as you quaintly call them, are usually of a reasonably harmless nature, Watson. I would not, for example, describe the dropping of a sandbag, with intent to kill or maim a distinguished comedian, as a jape, prank or practical joke. No, we are looking at something rather more serious, I feel. What puzzles me is that the dropping of the sandbag suggests a direct desire to harm Robey himself, but the other episodes appear to be designed to frighten and inconvenience, but not to inflict injury.'

As the interval loomed we decided to visit Robey in his dressing-room. Although it was perhaps forty minutes before his appearance was due, the comedian was in his sombre stage attire, which contrasted so strangely with his facial disguise, which verged upon the farcical; not quite the clown, but almost.

He rose from his seat before the dressing-room mirror to greet us. 'Went the day well, good sirs?'

There was a touch of the Shakespearean in his words. Holmes smiled and responded, 'Mr Robey, I have often heard that most comedians have a secret desire to play Hamlet. Is it one of your ambitions?'

Robey reacted as if Holmes had been the foil in a double act. 'In my early days I did play some small parts with a touring Shakespeare company. Ironically, I did once play the ghost of Hamlet's father. In fact I played such parts long enough for the experience to have left its permanent mark on my style of speech. I'll give you an example: only this morning I went into a tobacconist to buy some cigarettes. There were two girls standing behind the counter and I said to one of them, "Good morrow, good wench, hast thou amongst thy provender a brand which, whilst kind to my palate, will be yet kind to my purse strings?" '

I chuckled as I asked, 'And what was her reply, Mr Robey?'

He grinned widely. 'She turned to her friend and said,

"Oh blimee, Ada, get a packet of gaspers for King 'Enery the Heighth!" '

Even Sherlock Holmes was amused, saying, 'Mr Robey, it is neither Hamlet, nor yet Henry the Eighth that you should play, for you would make a really magnificent Falstaff!'

Robey mused, 'By Jove, sir, I believe that you are right! I shall bear your advice in mind. But come, sir, I feel sure that you do not wish to listen to my theatrical prattle. Have you any news for me concerning those things that you are investigating?'

We told him of our visit to the museum and our converse with the curator, and confirmed that the perfect copy of the Gelado which Robey himself had so painstakingly made reposed still in the show case masquerading as the real thing.

He was serious now. 'You advise me, then, to say nothing and let sleeping dogs lie?'

'I do indeed, sir, and I am anxious to discover if anyone would benefit from your death, aside from Mrs Robey and immediate family?'

'Mr Holmes, I hope to have a long career before me, one which may make me, eventually, a very wealthy man. But, at this moment in time, even my wife is better off with me alive. I live in a nice house as you have seen, surrounded by the things that I require for both survival and recreation, and most of what I earn is spent on maintaining these things. I am not a rich man, sir.'

I asked him, just to justify my existence, 'Where will you be next week, Mr Robey?'

The comedian made a gesture of mock pomposity. 'Next

week, Dr Watson, I will be what is referred to in the profession as "resting"! Oh yes, I may be a top-liner, but I am not always able to be in employment. However, the following week I will be taking myself off to Sheffield, and I have a fairly goodly run of music halls and variety houses thereafter. Gainful employment you might call it. So you see, all of next week my time is yours, gentlemen. I will co-operate with you as best I can.'

Holmes all but scared me with his next words. 'Mr Robey, we have four days to settle this matter of your Gelado and the theatre ghost. I do not wish to frighten you unduly, but I rely upon being able to bring it all to a satisfactory conclusion before the weekend. If I am unable to do so a very serious situation could result.'

Robey nodded, serious now. 'You think the two matters, the theatre ghost and the attempt upon my life, are connected?'

'Not entirely, sir, but I think whoever wishes you harm is taking advantage of the manifestations, psychic or mortal.'

'I will be guided by you, sir.'

'Good, now take my advice. Move about whilst you are on stage in order to frustrate any repeat of the affair with the sandbag. A moving target is a difficult one.'

Robey made a wry face. 'Oh, well, I mean to say, that would considerably alter the style of my performance, but I will try to do as you suggest. By Jove! The critics will sit up and say, "Old Robey has changed his act, after all these years!" You can watch from out front and tell me later how it seems to you.'

We promised to do so and were as good as our word, but

first Holmes had a few other matters to occupy his attention. He expressed a desire to talk with the stage doorkeeper and Robey told us that he was an old performer who had been in the business for a lifetime and was spending a semi-retirement in his present position.

'George Phelps used to call himself "The Encyclopaedic Wonder" because he had an incredible memory for dates and names, but times have changed and there is less demand for that curious type of turn; it has all speeded up now, you see. Still, George seems happy enough in his cubby-hole at the stage door.'

Mr Phelps proved to be a man of late middle-years and mournful appearance, yet with a brightness of manner which belied this.

He went out of his way to be helpful to Sherlock Holmes as soon as he had introduced himself, and said, 'Sherlock Holmes, born 1854, consulting detective, in practice since 1886, discovered new method of testing bloodstains . . .'

His threat to continue in this fashion caused Holmes to raise an admonishing hand and say, 'This is my friend and colleague, Dr John Watson . . .'

But this only changed the path of the torrent. 'Dr John H. Watson, MD, late of the British Army, served both in India and Afghanistan, invalided . . .'

It was my turn to stem the flow, 'Please, sir, we know a little about ourselves, it is your good self in which we are interested.'

But this too was a mistake on my part because he continued to talk like a reference volume, even concerning himself. 'George Augustus Phelps, born 1840, self-educated but discovered a talent for memorising facts, figures, names and places as early as 1850. Went on the music-hall stage . . .'

Holmes thought that he had found a way to stem the flow as he said, 'You know, Mr Phelps, if I had you at Baker Street I could dispense with my clutter of albums and reference works.'

But this did not do the trick either and Phelps droned on and on. 'Baker Street, a well-known London thoroughfare, can be traced back to Roman times when a track existed . . .'

Holmes drew me to one side, allowing Mr Phelps to continue with his monologue on Baker Street, and whispered to me, 'Watson, the man is impossible to engage in normal converse, so we must change our tactics and hope to gain something from his incredible memory. Follow my lead, if possible.'

My friend managed to interpolate a question when Phelps paused for breath, having given a two-minute discourse upon the subject of Baker Street. Holmes's tactics involved simply feeding Phelps with a name, dropping the niceties of polite conversation.

'Mary Malone.'

'Mary Malone, music-hall artiste, born 1838. Famous for the song "A-picking of the Daisies in the Park" and for her pert vivacity, which she started to lose through too much fondness for drink, around 1880. Said to have taken her own life following a performance at this very theatre in 1883. Believed to haunt the dressing-rooms and even the auditorium.'

I took Holmes's lead. 'George Robey?'

'Ah, George Robey, born George Edward Wade, actor turned music-hall comedian, making his ninth appearance at this theatre, the first having been in 1889 when he gained success with a song entitled "My 'at's a Brown 'un". The audience insisted upon singing the chorus all through several other acts which followed. Married, lives in the village of Finchley and is well known as a maker of violins . . .'

Holmes took up the cudgels again. 'Tom Elcott?'

'Thomas Elcott, born 1837, is said to have hung himself in dressing-room five of this very theatre on December the fourteenth, 1868, after being somewhat unsuccessful with a performance.'

I tried a direct question, 'Do you think that Tom Elcott is the theatre ghost?'

Holmes's eyes twinkled and I believe he had some idea of what might result from my question.

Certainly, as Phelps began to reply, I wished I had not asked it.

'Theatre ghosts: the Theatre Royal, Drury Lane, is said to be haunted by the ghost of Edmund Kean, whilst the spirit of David Garrick . . .' We had not time to see if he might ever get to the ghost of Murphy's House on the Green, so we politely made our farewells, leaving him still in full song, so to speak!

As we made again for the auditorium I remarked to my friend, 'That was a waste of time, was it not?'

But Holmes was not so sure. 'He is a strange man, Watson, probably not overburdened with intellect, yet with this freak ability to remember facts, even those most trivial. I imagine audiences found him interesting for a while, but he could, I think, grate on one's nerves and I'll wager his social life is somewhat limited. None the less, Watson, I can see that his talent to remember could be most useful to us.'

The theatre was not exactly packed, there being plenty of room in the pit, where we found a couple of seats at the end of a row where we could seat ourselves without causing discomfort or annoyance to others. We spotted old Murphy striding around at the back of the seating, appearing to be counting the number of patrons.

I remarked upon this to Holmes, who replied, 'Indeed he is "counting the house", as I believe it is called in theatrical parlance. The accident with the sandbag has put many people off attending this performance in a manner which the earlier so-called hauntings had failed to do. I wonder just who might benefit from his loss of business. A rival showman, perhaps? But then, I cannot believe that such a person would wish to take things as far as they have gone.'

'So this is what makes you think that the ghostly manifestations are unconnected with the attempt to harm Robey?'

'Certainly, and of course we have the added question of the mysterious exchange of violins. I cannot fit it all together, Watson. Why, even the sightings of the ghost seem to contradict each other concerning its sex, age and appearance. Maybe, if ghosts there be, we are dealing with three or four of them? Surely in such a case Murphy must own the most haunted theatre in history.'

Knowing Sherlock Holmes so well, I was surprised to hear him even consider actual hauntings being involved.

Of course he would always say that nothing should be discounted, but I knew in my heart that he had no sort of belief in the world of ghosts and spirits. I, myself, have ever had, and yet have a completely open mind upon the subject, and knew that despite Holmes's claims of such, his mind was really closed upon this subject. Sometimes I felt that this was a flaw in his character, but then I would remember the events surrounding one of his most famous cases. Whilst the rest of us had a fleeting belief in the existence of a spectral hound which roamed Dartmoor at night, intent upon the destruction of the Baskervilles, I know that Holmes had never believed that it was anything but a living beast. His complete lack of superstition had saved the life of Sir Henry and brought the rogue Stapleton to justice.

'Ah, here comes Robey, for his music is being played.'

Holmes had interrupted my reverie and drew my attention to the strains of 'Johnny's so Long at the Fair' played by the small band which Murphy always referred to as his 'orchestra'. The street scene descended and George Robey entered to a fair smattering of applause. The performer made his way to centre-stage and, having quietened the musicians, began his comical patter. But he had cleverly added an aspect to it.

He said, 'You will notice how I keep moving. Ha, ha! I'm no fool . . . makes me a more difficult target!'

The audience laughed, believing that he referred to missiles which might be thrown at him from the auditorium rather than anything from above. Then as Robey continued his comic quips he walked pointedly up and down, pausing first at one side of the stage and then at the other to deliver a *bon mot*, returning now and again to the centre for a minute or so. As he did this he leaned across the footlights and created an air of intimacy, as if trying to address everyone in the stalls personally. Moreover, he did not forget the circle and gallery, spasmodically stepping back and looking pointedly up at them.

He was in fact a merry fellow and noticing the sparsity of gallery patrons he said, 'I suppose on the mantelpiece they are all lying down? Ah well, I'm no critic of public behaviour!'

He was bright and breezy, risqué without a hint of being offensive, and this new mobile style obviously suited him. I felt that one had to take off one's hat to George Robey. No wonder people were beginning to call him 'The Prime Minister of Mirth'! My friend, doubtless, had similar views to mine, but was intent upon observation. However, nothing untoward had occurred when Robey was taking his final call. Then it happened! Between the street scene, against which Robey had performed, and the footlights there descended a scene depicting a woodland glade. The reader must appreciate that this did not descend slowly as had the street scene, but fell, rather like the blade of the guillotine beloved of the French Sûreté. There was a loud bang as its lowest wooden stretcher hit the boards of the stage. It missed Robey by inches, yet the audience scarcely realised this, and he recovered his composure so quickly that it had scarcely been lost. He removed his flat bowler as usual, to reveal the red-shock wig, and waved his cane in response to a healthy round of appreciation. As the strains of 'God Save the Queen' died away we were already making our way to the stage, in the belief that Her Majesty would have forgiven this seeming irreverence had she known its reason. The theatre curtain had descended and we clambered onto the stage, making our way through the centre curtain split to gain the area behind.

George Robey stood there, almost transfixed now, as if all his courage of the past moments had been spent.

He muttered to us, 'Upon my word, if they are so intent upon ending my existence, why do they not shoot me in the street or run me over with a horseless carriage? I mean to say!'

Holmes took his point at once. 'Mr Robey, your demise is intended to be an accident blamed upon the theatre ghost. This would cloud the waters and draw away the attention from a flesh-and-blood assassin. For that reason I believe you are safe except in the theatre itself.'

Robey was regaining his composure. 'I have always enjoyed appearing at Murphy's, but I'll admit that I will not be sorry when I have completed this week's work. Do you think I might be safe if I get away with my life until then?'

'Probably; until such time as you play another theatre with some sort of ghostly reputation, or some other aspect upon which your accidental demise could be blamed.'

Robey nodded wisely, completely understanding Holmes's suggested scenario. My friend decided not to climb into the flies, leaving this to Murphy's trusted flymen. This was not through any fear or indolence upon his part, but rather because he preferred to guard Robey's safety as he prepared to leave the theatre. We sat in the dressing-room whilst the comedian cleaned off his stage makeup and changed into his street clothes. Once more we marvelled at the transformation from buffoon to dagger English gentleman. Then we walked him to his carriage which awaited him at the stage door. I was surprised that Robey did not stay at the theatre between his two appearances, but he soon explained this.

'My agent has asked me to give an extra performance at the dear Old Met in the Edgware Road. It appears that Wilkie Bard is indisposed and he is short of a headline act. Marie filled in for him for the first house. I have ample time to get back here for my final appearance. Give you a chance to have a nose round, what?'

'Quite so, Mr Robey,' Holmes said, 'but I will send Dr Watson to Edgware Road with you, just in case this Old Met also has a ghost!'

As the carriage left I could hear the voice of George Phelps from the stage door. 'The Metropolitan Music Hall, Edgware Road, reputed to be London's oldest music hall . . .'

CHAPTER FOUR

The Met

I was quite surprised when we arrived at the Met to see that it appeared to be a rather splendid edifice compared to Murphy's. Surprised in the light of Phelps's parting remark that it was reputed to be London's oldest music hall.

But Robey enlightened me. 'There was an inn upon the site, built in 1525 and called "The White Hart". Eventually this inn developed a concert room and, later still, in 1864, it was transformed into the Metropolitan Music Hall, and only this year it has been refurbished to hail in the new variety. It is splendid outside, but just wait until you see the auditorium!'

Robey was right to enthuse, for as I sat in a front stall I admired the splendid theatre décor. Golden cherubs and other Grecian mythological figures abounded as embellishments to proscenium arch and supporting columns. Robey had told me that the transformation was all down to a brilliant architect, Frank Matcham, who specialised in designing and transforming music halls. The red-plush of the seating and the matching padding upon circle and gallery rails gave the house an appearance of opulence, and I imagine it helped the acoustics which were splendid.

I had missed the very beginning of the second house but I soon realised that I was watching a rather more expensive programme than that at Murphy's, with several headline acts on the one bill. Moreover, in place of the easel on which the current act numbers had rested there was a panel at each side of the stage where the numbers appeared by an ingenious system of electric light bulbs.

In fact, when Robey performed he took advantage of this, standing gazing into one of these panels and turning to the audience to say, 'Gosh, I have lost weight!'

Apart from this bit of extemporisation, his act was almost the same as I had seen at Murphy's, even to the newly-acquired walking up and down. This went well, so I suppose some good had come out of his seriously dangerous experiences. But I noticed that Robey's turn was somewhat shorter than I had seen before, and indeed there was a clockwork precision in what I saw of the rest of the show. The performing sea-lions were followed by an Irish tenor with a speed of continuity which scarce allowed the audience to show their appreciation of the clever aquatic animals and their maritime-clad trainer. I would have liked to have stayed at the Met for the entire performance, but I had only time to watch Colonel Pickering, the 'one-legged tap-dancer' (who explained to the audience that he had been champion clog dancer of Wigan before losing a leg in the Crimea), before Robey sent a call-boy to ask if I wished to remain or share his carriage back to the House on the

Green. I decided to go back to Murphy's with him in case Holmes needed my assistance.

As we travelled back I congratulated Robey upon his performance and remarked that there had been no hint of menace whilst he was at the Met.

His reply worried me a little. 'Dr Watson, I am beginning to think that my danger is entirely connected with Murphy's, and who knows, perhaps there is something in this ghost business after all?'

I hardly knew what to say, but tried to be as diplomatic as I possibly could. 'My dear Robey, Holmes and I have been connected with quite a number of cases where the supernatural appeared to be involved, but always the real solution eventually proved to be through entirely natural causes. Sherlock Holmes discounts nothing, but I know that secretly his mind is closed as far as the possibility of a ghost is concerned. Let us, though, consider for a moment or two the possibility of a ghostly visitation confined to the House on the Green. Assuming the place is haunted, why should the ghost wish you any possible harm? You are a man of even temperament and polite manner. I find it hard to believe that you have angered anyone, living or dead, to an extent that they would wish you such harm.'

Robey took a small, neat, spirit-flask from his pocket and offered it to me. I shook my head, and he took a draught from it himself.

His hand shook a little as he replaced the stopper. 'You can never tell in this business, Watson; you can upset fellow performers without intent or fault. There have been people I have shared bills with who resented that tiny bit more applause that it has so often been my good fortune to gain. With the new variety this is not quite so likely because the turns are presented with a continuity which does not allow many curtains to be taken, whereas with the old music halls, where the pace was more leisurely, it was different. If an audience liked a turn and demanded encore after encore, the management would be reluctant to deny them. Sometimes a less important act would have to wait until there was little time for them. Many is the time I have had to keep some poor trick cyclist or conjurer waiting in the wings, only to be denied an appearance.'

A point of logic occurred to me. 'But surely these people still got paid for their attendance, even if they could not appear, if the fault was not theirs?'

'Oh certainly, and if I was involved I always insisted upon that! But, my dear Watson, if you were yourself a performer you would understand what a nerve-wracking thing it is to build up your strength and nerve, as you do when expecting to perform, only to be left with that physical and nervous energy unexploded. Surely, as a medical man, you can understand this?'

'Why, yes, Robey, I think I can understand your point exactly. During the Afghan campaign I can remember men who had been worked up to a fever pitch, ready to go into battle, only to have their orders changed. Often during the hours that followed they would relieve their tension by quarrelling among themselves.'

'Ah, so you do understand completely; well, imagine how much harder these circumstances would be whilst one is still endeavouring to make a name for oneself. I can remember even now an incident of such a nature which occurred at Collins's music hall at Islington about five years ago. A poor fellow, who called himself Karno or Karmo, or some such, was held in the wings whilst I took encore after encore, so that he had to rush through his act and rather spoiled it in the process. He was a protean artiste, you know, a quick-change act, played a sketch all on his own making lightning changes from one character to another. The heroine, the hero, the villain, the sailor, you know the sort of thing. Well, he had several agents out front to see him perform and made a poor showing for them. I don't suppose he forgave me for a long time.'

'What happened to him?'

'I don't know, I have never appeared on a bill with him since, but I feel sure that he did well eventually because he had a good act.'

'Through the years have you upset any other performers? For example, a trapeze acrobat, or a singer called Mary Malone?'

'Few, I imagine, and certainly not those that you mention.'

I felt that I had developed a few trains of thought for Sherlock Holmes to consider as we reached the House on the Green, but there was no time for Robey to gossip more with me as he was due at the theatre to prepare for his second house appearance. I ventured to ask him why he had bothered to clean off his makeup and change into his street clothes when he only had to go through the whole procedure in his dressing-room.

His reply was interesting. 'My dear Doctor, to be seen in

your stage characterisation by the public, save by the audience you entertain on stage, is unprofessional. Many an act has been dismissed just for visiting the theatre bar during the interval in costume and makeup. It's just not done, my dear fellow!'

I was learning all the time, learning the etiquette and deportment demanded of this, as of any other, profession. After all, I mused, a surgeon would not walk the streets or travel by carriage in the robes he wore when operating.

Holmes greeted me eagerly on my arrival. 'You have missed some excitement, Watson. This time it was Miss Marie Lloyd who experienced the inconvenience of the breakdown of the electric lights. But more, during the resulting darkness a sinister-looking apparition appeared upon the stage and was seen by the entire audience!'

'Upon my word! What form did it take?'

'Oh, it was a fairly conventional ghost, if such there be; a luminescent, draped figure with a white face, its jaw supported by a white cloth. Very sinister and terrifying to the superstitious. A great many women ran screaming from the theatre. However, all is calm now. I have investigated the fuses and they had simply been interfered with. As for the ghost, well, I have discovered traces of phosphorus upon some of the scenic flats, where the so-called ghost made accidental contact.'

Despite his having used the term 'excitement', Holmes himself was far from excited. Indeed I have seldom known him to be so calm. He forestalled further questions by asking for an account of my visit to the Met. I had little to report.

'The theatre is rather splendid when compared to this one. Robey experienced no inconvenience and was well received by the audience, but I fear, Holmes, that this whole situation is beginning to affect his nerve. Perhaps, if you tell him about the phosphorus it will quieten him.'

We stood in the wings to await Robey, who we knew must soon arrive there. When he did I noticed a strong smell of spirits and, even through his thick theatrical coloration, one could sense the anxiety in his face.

'Holmes, Watson, I have just heard of the events which occurred during the excursion to the Met! Can you still believe, Doctor, in the non-existence of ghostly visitors?'

I tried to reassure him. 'I think my friend has some news that you have perhaps not heard yet.'

As Holmes imparted the news of the phosphorus, Robey calmed considerably. 'So, you are right to think that perhaps someone is playing ghost. But why does he play harmless pranks except when he deals with me?'

Holmes tried to explain. 'I believe we are dealing with two or more persons playing ghost. Of course, you might insist that we are dealing with a real ghost as well, but I rather doubt it. Robey, be assured that I have positioned observers in the flies and backstage, so I imagine that it would be safe enough for you to enjoy entertaining your audience unharried by mortals.'

As he spoke, Robey's opening music began to play so, using the official means of entering the auditorium from behind the scenes, we went through the pass door and stood in a side aisle to watch.

'Is it safe to leave him thus?' I whispered.

Holmes nodded and whispered, 'I believe he is well guarded, Watson.'

To the audience I feel sure that George Robey seemed as amusing and casual as ever, but I felt that I could detect that anxiety still in his manner. He missed out a line that I remembered from his patter and a cue that he should have given the conductor. This resulted in his starting one of his songs a little in advance of the band, but it was soon adapted and all was well. Then, just as he was walking towards the right-hand wing to make his final exit, it happened. A knife, thrown from where I knew not, whisked through the air and, missing him by inches, landed embedding itself in a feature of the design on the proscenium arch. As it quivered there an audible gasp came from the audience and George Robey froze, standing there like one of the statuettes of himself which could be purchased in the lobby!

Holmes was the first to reach the missile and I was the first to be at Robey's side. 'All is well, Robey. Let me take you to your dressing-room.'

He shook his head, wanting to learn something of our actions. Holmes gauged the angle of throw and disappeared into the opposite wing as the band played the National Anthem.

As the audience departed they illustrated my long-held regard for the inherent kindness of the average resident of the greatest and biggest city in the world. There were cries of 'Good old George!' and 'Watch out, George . . . mind yourself, Cully!' They gave me the impression that most of them wanted to stay, yet not through idle curiosity, rather from a real concern for the safety and well-being of a favourite entertainer.

I walked over, and through to the backstage area, joining Holmes who was talking to the stage manager. 'You say that you saw no one, yet fancied you heard a swish of draperies an instant following the thud of the knife on the proscenium arch?'

'Yes, sir, but I saw nothing before that. Mind you, I was busy with the house tabs.'

'House tabs?'

'Yes, Mr Holmes, that's what we call the front curtains. I was making ready to lower them for the end of Mr Robey's turn.'

Holmes moved back a little and stood looking towards the proscenium arch.

'He would have been standing roughly where I am now in order to throw the knife?'

The stage manager shook his head.

'I would have seen him, although it might be a trifle dim back here, what with the black drapes and all. The stage is lit bright but not a lot of that light filters through to here.'

We insisted, as soon as we had made a perfunctory search around the backstage area, on accompanying George Robey back to his home. As we left in the carriage, I tried to make small talk. 'That dome on Murphy's is quite a height, is it not? I had not realised how high it was before.'

Robey, although obviously more concerned with his own problem, was gentleman enough to reply. 'Yes, it must be at least sixty feet high.'

Holmes looked at the dome as if noticing it for the first

time. His keen eye gave the answer, 'More like seventy.'

Then my friend seemed to descend into his own thoughts, as did Robey, leaving me to my own thoughts and devices. None of us spoke until we reached the Robey house, where we accepted a late nightcap before returning to Baker Street. This we did after Holmes had reassured Robey that he was safe enough, save at Murphy's.

I was puzzled by this, knowing that Holmes was disinclined to believe the hauntings as anything but man-made. Therefore, why would the human agent who wished to harm Robey not do so wherever he happened to be? Could I have been wrong and did Holmes consider some possibility in a spiritual attacker that could operate only within the precincts of the House on the Green?

As we sat by the fire at Baker Street for a final smoke, I dared broach the subject. 'So is a ghost then at Murphy's?'

'Yes, or rather three of them, at least; we have had very convincing accounts of sightings by a number of sensible people. We have, moreover, been able from these accounts to even name them . . .'

I was amazed at what I heard from my friend, and enquired, rather tentatively, 'This *is* the same Sherlock Holmes that I have known so well for so many years . . . or at least, thought I did?'

'The very same, my dear Watson, the very same. But when I refer in this instance to ghosts, I do not mean those of the ethereal variety. We are looking for two or three men and a woman who have been playing ghost at Murphy's.'

'I see . . . but what could be their motive in trying to kill George Robey?'

'As I see it, Watson, the "ghosts" work in close collabora-tion, their main motive being to ruin Murphy and his theatre. All of them have some connection, no doubt, with those persons who have died within those walls, through circumstances which may, or they may think, have been through Murphy's actions. With this in mind they have tried to gain the building a bad reputation as being haunted. When this did not do more than reduce attendances by a fraction, they decided that something of a more serious nature was needed, such as the actual death of a headline performer.'

I began to understand his train of thought. 'They are all carrying out personal vendettas, then?'

'It would seem so, Watson, but of course my theories are as yet full of holes. This is a four-pipe problem, to be sure. Possibly, when we meet again at breakfast, I will be able to tell you more. Perhaps before you retire you could pass to me those albums and folios which are lying in such a neat pile upon that shelf.'

I picked up the pile of folios and noted that there were old theatrical journals, and a slim volume titled *The Who's Who of Vaudeville* among them. He took these from me and carelessly threw them upon the floor about him as he sank upon the fireside rug and started to refill his pipe. I could see that his night would be long and thoughtful.

I was tired and slept heavily, arising at a somewhat late hour to find that Holmes had disposed of his breakfast and, looking extremely sharp and cleanly shaven, he shot me an accusing look. 'Watson, I have spent the night in deep thought and had hoped that you might be the first to hear of any conclusions that I had leapt to, or at least reached.'

I muttered some apologies, brushing over my tardiness by saying, 'Am I to believe then that you did in fact reach a conclusion and that it will advance your progress in the case of George Robey and the House on the Green?'

'I hinted last night that we could be dealing with two matters which simply appeared to have a connection. But I have decided that I was wrong in thinking that we are looking at several ghosts.'

'Then how do you explain their quite dissimilar appearances and even different sexes?'

Holmes was serious now as he leaned forward and spoke to me quietly but earnestly. 'Watson, within the pages of those professional journals, I read with very great interest concerning a branch of the vaudevillian art known as that of the "protean artiste". I found accounts, for example, of such an artiste, one Castelli, who performed complete one-act plays or excerpts from those of full length, playing all the parts himself, both male and female. For example, he would perform a scene from Dickens's masterpiece, *Oliver Twist*, titled "The Death of Nancy". In this, during the time allotted to a variety act, he not only impersonated Sykes, Nancy and Fagin, but made frequent changes of costume and makeup, literally within seconds and without any sort of stage waits that were not natural to the piece. Our man who plays at ghosts could be such an artiste; indeed for him it would have been far easier than having to make his nerve-wrack-ing transformations. I believe I know just where to find further information that could be of value. Come, Watson, we will take ourselves yet again to the House on the Green.'

'But, Holmes, my breakfast!'

'Just think, Watson, you had an extra hour in bed; surely you have learned by now that one cannot have everything in this life. Seriously, my dear fellow, I have no doubt we can remedy the pleadings of your inner man before an hour or two has passed.'

Within half an hour we were again standing outside the old theatre which was becoming as familiar to my friend as it had been to me.

He glanced up at the dome and remarked. 'I have given thought to your remark of last night regarding the height of Murphy's dome. But more of that anon, we have other more pressing affairs to investigate.'

The way he flew from topic to topic was quite surprising, but then Sherlock Holmes was a law unto himself. He made for the stage door, knowing by now from experience that it was open, and manned for an hour or two in the morning. The stage doorman gets his leisure time in the middle of the day rather than at the end of it.

'Mr Phelps, what can you tell me of an artiste known as Castelli?' Holmes gently handed the cue to the memory-gifted stage doorkeeper. The answer was instant and animated. 'Castelli, "Protean actor extraordinaire", born Hastings, Sussex, April 4th, 1840. Successful in a modest way, until the night in November of 1897 when he had a disastrous performance at this very theatre which virtually ended his career.'

This answer evidently interested my friend, who asked, 'Can one bad performance ruin a variety artiste's career?'

Phelps, a little to my surprise, dropped his memory-wonder persona for a few minutes and explained rather earnestly, 'As a rule, no; such things can be quickly forgotten, save where a showcase is concerned!'

'What is a showcase?' I asked.

'Well, sir, it is a week at a theatre where a performer, even an established one, tries out a new act. Usually he will send passes to all the big booking agents and impresarios, that they may judge for themselves and book him accordingly. Quite often the artiste will appear for a greatly reduced salary in order to be able to present an act which has not yet been seen. It is a risk for both artiste and management. But when a claque is involved it can turn a bit nasty!'

I was bewildered.

'A claque?'

It was Holmes who replied, 'I am familiar with the term, Phelps; it is an organised group of persons who attend a theatre to cheer and applaud a particular performer, is it not?'

'Why, yes, sir, that is the general idea. But sometimes it works in reverse. A rival or an ill-wisher can organise a group to go into a theatre and boo a certain performer, even throw things at him.'

'This happened to Castelli at this theatre?'

'Yes, sir it was highly organised, and the whole thing ended in bad blood between old Murphy senior and Castelli. The artiste had been swanking around rather and asking for more than Murphy thought he was worth, so he offered him a showcase and there were those who thought that Murphy organised the claque with the idea of forcing his price down. Anyway, it ruined Castelli and quite broke his nerve.'

Holmes pressed a half sovereign upon Phelps who was quite overwhelmed by his generosity. 'Oh, sir, Mr Holmes, how kind. Please feel free to ask me any more questions whenever you wish . . .'

As we hurried into the theatre and wandered onto the stage, my friend turned to me with something like triumph in his expression. 'Well, Watson, I believe we have at last made some sort of breakthrough towards laying the ghost of the House on the Green. Castelli had the motive and the ability to play three or four different ghosts. Perhaps Murphy can throw more light upon this aspect?'

We found Murphy, with his cronies, in the bar as usual. He was affable in a stern sort of way. Grim good humour, I suppose, would describe his manner towards us.

'Well, gentlemen, you have been at it a day or two now. Anything to report that might cheer me?'

Holmes led Murphy to an as yet unoccupied table that we might gain some measure of intimacy.

'My dear Murphy, does the name Castelli mean anything to you?'

'The quick-change artiste? Why, yes, I have heard of him; but not for a long time. He appeared here years ago during my dad's time, but I don't remember seeing him.'

'Is it true that there was some bad blood between Castelli and your father?'

'Oh no, I'm sure not; you don't want to listen to theatrical gossip. Why, I believe my father even gave him a special showcase week . . .'

His manner became a little guarded as he continued, '. . . if he didn't make good use of the facilities offered him it was his bad luck. Anyway, I heard that he went to Australia and made quite a success afterwards.'

'Can you be sure of that?'

'No, I can't, but that's what I heard.'

I could tell that Holmes realised that he would gain little by pressing the point, so he changed his tactics slightly. 'Quite so; just another enquiry or two. Is there among your permanent employees anyone who might consider he has more class than his job would normally entail?'

Murphy's manner changed from slightly furtive to downright peevish. 'Too much class? I can't imagine what you mean, sir! Why to work at the House on the Green is an honour. All my staff, front of house and back, are chosen for their smartness and ability.'

Holmes rephrased his question with great diplomacy. 'Let me put it another way, my dear Murphy; who would you consider to be the very smartest of your male employees?'

He was thoughtful for a while, then said, 'Well, old Grimes, the front-of-house doorman, is probably the most immaculate. Always very smart, his uniform neatly pressed. He always gives the patrons a good impression as he stands outside and salutes the regulars.'

'What are his duties during the performances themselves?'

'Oh, not a lot; as I say, he stands outside as the people enter and when they leave. There are a couple of assistant doormen who see to things the rest of the time. Old

Grimes is a figurehead really. He has a changing-room, not much more than a cupboard really, just behind the stage boxes on the right-hand side of the auditorium.'

'Who has keys to this apartment?'

'Grimes, of course, and I think there is one on the big ring in my office.'

'What do you suppose Grimes does to occupy himself during the hour or two each night that he occupies that place?'

Murphy was puzzled. 'I don't know, sinks the odd pint, I daresay, and probably spends a bit of time polishing his buttons and pressing his trousers, if appearances are anything to go by. What else was it? You said a couple of things.'

Holmes surprised me again with his reply. 'Watson has noticed that the dome of this building is rather higher than we at first thought it to be, judging from the inside view. Have you any comment to make upon this?'

It seemed equally surprising, this comment and question, to Murphy as it was to myself, but he answered glibly enough. 'The original building had a far smaller stage and the dome was over part of the front stalls. It had a moving panel which could be opened on summer nights, or between houses to make the smoke less dense. Then, when the stage itself was extended, of course the dome was right over it and it was blocked off. The builders, in their wisdom, decided to make a false top so that the dome was more of a feature outside, to make up for its lack of use inside.'

I confess that I was surprised at how seriously Holmes had evidently taken my observation concerning the dome which had been spoken in a manner that had bordered upon the making of conversation. But the more I thought about it the more I felt that I knew what might be in Holmes's mind. There could be, I thought, a secret compartment, where someone who liked to play ghost could hide and await his opportunities. I was puzzled, however, by Holmes's interest in the theatre front-of-house doorman who seemed an unlikely candidate for any sort of wrongdoing. However, I kept my own counsel concerning these thoughts and awaited my friend's lead.

However, we were distracted by the unexpected arrival of George Robey who entered the bar briskly and joined us at the table. His manner belied, I felt, his real feelings of apprehension. He put down his hat and cane and stood there, immaculate, looking as little like a music-hall comedian as might be thought possible. He spoke with an air of bonhomie, for the benefit of Murphy, I felt. 'A real little crowd of conspirators, eh what? I mean to say!'

Murphy rose and made to move towards the bar. 'George! What will you have?'

'My word, is the sun over the yard-arm? No matter, just this once I'll have a sherry wine, and blow all my good resolutions!'

I wondered if he had information to impart, but said nothing in case it might be something for our ears only and not for those of the theatre owner.

Holmes offered the chance for a private chat by saying, 'By the bye, my dear Robey, I would like to discuss something with you. Is your dressing-room available?'

Murphy expressed mock pique, saying, 'Oh, well, if my

employees don't enjoy my company and have secrets to discuss! Speaking of employment, Holmes, I really will expect some progress soon, before I am ruined by that wretched spectre.'

To my surprise, Holmes reassured him, 'I believe your problem will be solved before the week is out, Murphy. My meeting with Mr Robey is closely connected to my efforts. You are indeed the founder of the feast and, as such, will be shown the greatest respect; but, as Watson will tell you, I have my methods.'

As we made towards the dressing-rooms, Robey said, 'I don't want you to take this amiss, Holmes, but I came down here at this hour in the hope of doing a little detective work myself. I know you advised me to keep to my home ground except for the performances, but, well to be honest, I have been getting restless. I mean to say . . .'

Holmes smiled enigmatically and said to me, 'You see, Watson, all my clients are losing their confidence in me. Old Murphy is getting impatient, now Mr Robey here is getting restless, and I have not yet solved the enigma of Mrs Beadle's missing pug-dog.'

Robey made efforts to reassure Holmes that his actions were simply prompted by anxiety, whilst I gazed at him blankly as I said, 'I know nothing of a Mrs Beadle, or a missing pug-dog!'

My friend emitted a rare laugh, 'If you could develop the habit of rising earlier, Watson, you might know more about the elusive canine and several other matters with which I am presently concerned; for example, the bishop's ring, and the talking parrot which alone knows a certain coded limerick which will solve an important mysterious matter.'

I merely grunted. Had I not known Holmes better I would have thought that he was 'pulling my leg', as we used to say in the army. But I knew that he did not lean towards childish japes. Certainly my tardiness in rising could be depriving me of a wealth of minor mysteries so I vowed to make the effort to become an early riser. But as Robey sprung his dressing-room lock, there were sounds of a scuffle from within and Holmes pushed us both aside, then thrusting the door open, he leapt into the room. We followed him swiftly but the room was empty, save for Holmes's presence as he leant through the partly open sash window. I rushed to his side but could see that we were too late to catch the intruder.

Holmes said as much. 'A second or two earlier, Watson, and we might have grabbed him. I say "him" because I cannot quite picture a woman taking part in such activity, although he was as slight as a female.'

'How do you know that?'

'My dear Watson, could *you* escape through that very small aperture?'

I took his point; I had to agree that I could not, or if I could, certainly not so speedily. At best I might have forced my way through, *sans* greatcoat and jacket but only then with a great effort, and slowly at that. I was considering if someone of Holmes's build might have managed it, when he answered my unspoken question by thrusting himself through the open portion of the window. He did it cleanly enough but with a certain degree of hesitance. More easily he managed the twelve-foot drop to the paved alley below.

I hung through the window to converse with him. 'Shall you pursue him, Holmes?'

'Good heavens, no, Watson, the bird has well and truly flown! I made the drop just to ascertain his degree of fitness. Certainly it must have been equal to my own.'

'Shall you return through the stage door?'

'If I must, though first I will see if it is possible for me to gain an entry from where I stand.'

It was not long before Holmes had answered his own question, as his long, slim fingers appeared upon the window sill, closely followed by his great beak of a nose. He warned me off as I attempted to assist him, demonstrating that he could gain entry, perhaps not with ease, but yet without great difficulty. As he stood beside us in the dressing-room he brushed down his jacket with his hands.

'How did you climb back, Holmes, is there a drain pipe?'

'No, Watson, but the window is of the bay kind and, therefore, there is a corner of brickwork. Normally it would not help but in this particular instance it is decorative, with every other corner brick protruding slightly. To the adroit it is a ladder.' Robey was businesslike as usual. 'So, Holmes, we are seeking a slim, active man, which could describe about an eighth of the male adult population of London?'

Holmes smiled admiringly at the comedian's logic. 'Quite so, but it is somewhere to start from and you can get nowhere at all unless you make a start, my dear Robey. Let us look about us for other useful pieces of information. The brick dust which adhered to his boots, as it has to mine, has given us a splendid set of footprints. He walked lightly, and has small feet. The soles of his boots were sewn there by hand, so we are not dealing with a passing sneak-thief.'

I chimed in, and was to regret it. 'Unless he wore the boots discarded by a well-to-do man?'

Holmes smiled and spoke ironically. 'Robey will, perhaps, tell us what the chances are of a man with such small feet finding the discarded footwear of another with similar pedal extremities.'

Thus, he had turned his irony upon both Robey and me in the same utterance. But his eyes and hands were busy as he spotted and lifted a small sheet of paper from the makeup desk. 'What do you make of this, Watson? You know my methods well enough by now. Describe the person who wrote this note.'

I looked at the epistle with interest, and noted that it had been written in pencil with a rather thick lead. Indeed I got the impression that it might have been written with a theatrical pencil of the kind intended to emphasise eyebrows or moustaches, but Holmes soon contradicted this theory. 'It is written with an artist's crayon, Watson. The paper has taken it as would be expected. Mr Robey will doubtless find you a makeup stick of the kind you have mentioned. If you apply it to paper you will see that it will produce a film rather than an accepted mark. We may well be dealing with a person of artistic inclination. Now let us consider the wording. He read the message aloud, that we might hear it . . .

HAS THAT WRETCHED THING APPEARED AGAIN? 'TWILL BE YOUR DEATH!

Robey shrugged and, glancing around him, said, 'Nothing has been stolen, so he just meant to scare me with his allusion to the ghost.'

'He could be an actor, for he quotes from Shakespeare,' I ventured.

'I doubt it,' Robey replied, 'for an actor would be correct in his quotation. It is from *Hamlet*, and it does refer to the ghost in its correct form; that of Hamlet's father. We are looking at a man of education, and taking Holmes's point regarding the pencil, one with at least a passing interest in art.'

Holmes was delighted. 'Splendid, my dear Robey, we will make a detective of you yet! You will have realised, also, that the writer of this note had visited you in your dressing-room, either here or at some other theatre.'

Robey and I glanced at each other; we could not follow this train of thought.

He explained. 'The intruder wrote his note, or threat, upon the top sheet of a pad which you keep beside your makeup box.'

'Correct, I keep the pad there always that I may scribble notes for the call-boy to fetch tea, coffee and the like, or a sandwich during the interval. I place the money beside the pad so if I am on stage or elsewhere, he can take the note and the money. We are allowed to have snacks brought in, but fried fish is banned backstage at most theatres because of the smell.'

'So he knew, this intruder, that he would find that pad, and not need to bring his own, or an already written message. He knows your methods, Robey, just as Watson knows mine; though he does not need to be a colleague or confidant to know such a thing.'

'Agreed, but it does narrow the field a little, Holmes. After all, I can tell you that only a few people visit me in my dressing-room. If my admirers wish to speak with me I tend to go down to the stage door to deal with them. I could count my visitors for the last six months on the fingers of one hand.'

'And these are, for example?'

'Well, aside from my lady wife, there would be my agent, who would hardly benefit from harming me in any way. My cousin, Charlie, a maiden aunt, Martha, and the artist, Phil May, who came once or twice to sketch me for a portrait.'

'Can this portrait be seen anywhere?'

'I can show you a reproduction of it. I had a plate made to reproduce it for the back of my professional card.'

He produced a card from his jacket, like a conjurer producing a chosen pasteboard.

Holmes studied it and smiled. 'An excellent caricature by a brilliant artist. I know Mr May quite well and I am convinced that he would not be a suitable suspect despite the original having clearly been in black crayon. But just to put your minds at rest, let me point out that Mr May is quite a large man with equally proportionate feet.'

'Why, Holmes, it would never have occurred to me to suspect Phil, even if he had fulfilled all the specifications of evil that you have concocted. I would be more likely to suspect my maiden aunt. Oh, by the way, my solicitor was a visitor too, for I have thought it a good idea to make my will. But this would have been several months ago. He, at least, is above suspicion.'

Holmes took out his hunter, opened and studied it. 'Watson, I have a few minor investigations to make here, and I also need to consult further with friend Robey. Now, I have an errand which I would ask you to perform for me and, as it is a matter of the utmost delicacy, I would be most grateful if you could see your way to performing it.'

'Holmes, you know I will help in any way I can.'

'My dear fellow, I know, but this is an imposition as it requires a journey to Reigate in Surrey. If you hurry to Victoria you can catch the train at three of the clock. Here is a note which you must deliver by hand to the person and address written upon the envelope. He will hand you a package or box of some kind which you should insist upon before actually handing the envelope to him. I know I can rely upon you.'

'Consider it done, Holmes; shall you be here or at Baker Street when I return?'

'Here, Watson, I will await your return, however long it takes you.'

CHAPTER FIVE

My Errand to Reigate

I managed to miss the three o'clock train and had to wait a further hour to catch another which stopped there, so by the time I was actually in Reigate itself, it was nearer to five than to four. I had, of course, already studied the name and address on the envelope that I was to deliver, and was soon in a cab with the driver urging his quadruped in the direction of Miller's Farm. We arrived eventually at what I can only describe as a smallholding, a mile or two south of Reigate itself, in what one can only call an almost rural situation. Newly-built houses appeared to be making infiltration into the countryside where crumbling barns and once prosperous farmhouses stood, grown over with vegetation and neglect. Miller's Farm proved to be such a location and a knock upon the front door of this, perhaps once imposing edifice, produced a series of barks and yaps. An uncouth-looking individual at length answered my knock and agreed that he might indeed be Joshua Flood, to whom the envelope was addressed. He was as uncouth in speech as in manner and appearance.

'Yus, wotcher want?'

'If you are Joshua Flood, I have this envelope to give you from Sherlock Holmes; but he told me to take charge of a box or basket before handing it to you.'

He disappeared for perhaps thirty seconds and then reappeared carrying a basket rather like a small hamper, with a leather carrying strap. I took this from him and handed him the envelope. The fact that I knew not if I was expected to await his opening it and making some sort of reply, was made irrelevant by his slamming of the door. I carried the basket to the cab and bade the driver to return me to the railway station. In fact, it was not until I had got myself and the basket upon a Victoria-bound train, that I thought of the possibility of examining the contents of it.

I had heard some sounds of movement from inside and gathered that some kind of live creature, or creatures, were within. No barks or mews emitted, just the odd sniff and snuffle. I tried to make out what was within by peering closely through the basketwork which proved to be too closely woven to permit this. I toyed with the securing strap and buckle but thought better of unfastening it and opening the lid. If whatever was inside escaped into the railway carriage, it might be more than my life was worth to have to explain to Holmes that I had lost his . . . (I still had no idea what) on the Reigate to Victoria train!

Indeed, I spent the rest of the journey trying to deduce just what might lurk within. What sort of a live creature might Holmes require for the work upon which he was presently engaged? No sort of dog large enough to be of any use to a detective could be contained within those wicker confines. Perhaps it was a ferret, or several ferrets, trained in the art of ghost hunting? At one of the stations we stopped at, an old woman got into my carriage and, despite the legend 'smoking' which was etched upon the glass, complained of my pipe.

I pointed out the notice, but this did not pacify her. 'To make it worse, sir, you are travelling with a live creature which could, I feel sure, be irritated by the fumes from that wretched pipe of yours. If it is a parrot it could contract bronchitis or if it is a cat it could get a colic. What is it that you have in the basket? I can hear it move but it makes no utterances.'

I did not feel like telling that I knew not what it was, so I told her that it was a creature not, as yet, classified by science.

She was most intrigued. 'How very interesting, did you discover it yourself?'

'Yes, on my last expedition to Patagonia.'

'Fascinating! May one be permitted to see it?'

'Oh no, I fear it is extremely dangerous. Despite its compact size it is a man-eating creature and at present it is very hungry indeed.'

'Can you then, perhaps, describe it?'

'Certainly. It is about the size of a large polecat, but has a head much out of proportion to its body, a wide mouth and a set of needle-sharp teeth. It lives in a steamy jungle and, in order that it should feel at home, I am forced to smoke this strong tobacco to produce fumes that will pacify it.'

'Oh I see; I thought you seemed too much of a gentleman to be smoking that wretched thing for your own satisfaction.'

'Yes, madam, I am a martyr to science. The fumes displease me, but I must keep the animal alive until I can placed it in the specially-built greenhouse I have prepared for it!'

As the reader will know, I am not in the habit of speaking deliberate untruths, especially to elderly ladies, but in this particular instance I felt that making an exception did no harm. More, it even did a certain amount of good in preserving good relations and giving the dear woman something to tell her friends at the sewing circle!

I deposited the basket at Baker Street on my way back to the House on the Green, which I reached during the interval. Holmes was in the entrance lobby smoking a foul clay which would have sent the old lady on the train into a fit; but at least he was not inflicting it upon the patrons of Murphy's establishment. He greeted me in his usual crablike manner, as if approaching from one side.

'Watson! I have some very bad news to impart; friend Robey was struck by another sandbag from the flies and I fear that he is dead. Oh, by the way, did you manage to collect the basket without difficulty? Flood can be a difficult customer sometimes.'

To say that I was appalled by his cavalier manner in so roughly breaking the news of the tragedy is to put it very mildly indeed.

I spoke, I fear, rather sharply to my friend. 'Never mind the wretched basket! What happened exactly?'

'I fear I had left the auditorium to investigate the closet

used by the doorman, when I heard this thud, followed by gasps and then a shocked silence. Soon the band were playing merrily and old Murphy was on the stage reassuring the audience that, despite a slight accident, all was well, and they left the theatre, muttering, but otherwise very quietly indeed. It seems that the curtain had closed and Robey was about to take his call when it happened. He was killed outright and suffered not at all; but I have plans afoot to apprehend his assassin before this night is out.'

I was still shaken, and said, 'That will be very little comfort to Mrs Robey. Tell me, has she been informed?'

'Not yet, nor has his death been made public, save to one or two persons. I have a plan that the killer might implicate himself. Robey is resting now at an undertaker's establishment nearby whither we will go directly. I warn you to keep silent concerning the whole matter, Watson, until I confirm that you may relax your guard.'

'But, Holmes, he is a famous artiste and well-liked. You cannot for long keep his death a secret.'

'True, but for a few hours the news will be kept from the public. For the present, Murphy has, on my instruction, posted a notice on the ticket office to the effect that Mr Robey is not appearing through circumstances beyond the control of the management. We will now take ourselves to the undertakers and I will tell you a few more details of what I have done since you left for Reigate.'

I was still in a kind of daze as we travelled by hansom to the address which Holmes had given the cabby. I was anxious to hear more despite my bewilderment.

Holmes enlarged on what had happened. 'Robey had

arrived early in order to give me a copy of his will, which I had requested. I studied this and from it learned which persons would benefit from his demise. I have, so far, had these persons informed and no others. They will be visiting the undertakers and I feel that I will learn something from one of them to confirm my suspicions. By the way, the doorman is, as we suspected, playing ghost. I have confronted him and he has admitted as much to me. You see, I opened up his closet whilst he was performing his duties in front of the theatre. I found, therein, the costumes and makeup materials which would have enabled such a skilled quick-change artiste as himself to impersonate at least three or four different shades! By the way, he admitted to me that he had once been the famous Castelli, and that Murphy, the elder, had all but ruined him by hiring a claque to boo and taunt him on that historic occasion.'

'Good heavens, why would old Murphy want to do that?'

'Oh, just to force down the price of the protean artiste's services. I do not believe he wished to finish his career.'

'That was Murphy senior; why should Castelli want to take it out upon his son?'

'Who knows what thoughts can haunt the minds of troubled men, Watson? I believe that he would have hesitated to try to deceive the older theatre owner with a dual personality. Once old Murphy had gone he saw his chance, and I suppose the very name of the theatre still enraged him.'

'Did you have him arrested?'

'Good heavens, no! What is more, I gained a form of pardon from Murphy for Castelli, assuming that the hauntings cease forthwith. The man is troubled but there is no evil in him. I believe the poor man can be redeemed; but more of that later, for come, we have reached the under-takers.'

Indeed we had, and we alighted from the hansom out-side a rather dingy-looking, heavily-draped shop window with a small hand-painted notice standing in it which proclaimed 'Jarvis and Sons, Funeral Undertakers'.

'Come along, Watson, there is no time to waste, the game is afoot . . .'

I found the familiar Holmesian phrase a little out of place. After all, I mused, poor old Robey was already dead, so there seemed little cause to hurry!

'Have any of the visitors arrived?'

'No, sir, no mourners as yet.'

This dialogue between the undertaker and Sherlock Holmes also had a slight ring of the macabre. Was I dream-ing all this? I still could not fully accept all that Holmes had told me.

But then he began to make at least a little more sense of his actions as he said, 'Watson, beyond that door George Robey lies in his coffin. On each side of the apartment are draped alcoves, in one of which I suggest we secrete our-selves and contrive to study the reactions of the several persons who will shortly arrive to view the body. One of them may, in this way, tempt the finger of accusation!'

I was still uncomfortable about the whole thing; there seemed a ring of undue haste and unreality about the whole affair. However, my friend would not be further drawn and he opened the door to the apartment where Robey lay with,

I thought, irreverent style, making no attempt to curb the sounds of his movements or footfalls. It seemed a bit pointless for me to creep in behind him, but old habits die hard. As we passed the coffin *en route* for the curtained alcove which Holmes indicated, I cast a quick glance at the body which reclined within. If I had thought everything thus far to be a trifle unreal, imagine my shock upon seeing that Robey was lying there in his full stage costume and makeup.

I began to protest at such lack of taste, but Holmes quietened me by saying, 'Watson, there will be a post-mortem examination, until when all must be left as it is.'

He bundled me into the alcove and made sure that we were hidden by the heavy curtains. Holmes held a curtain aside long enough to study his hunter and then carefully rearranged it, saying, 'We should not be kept waiting long now.'

He was right for, I judged, within ten minutes there were sounds of an arrival, and by very carefully peering through a tiny space between the drapes, I espied a woman, heavily veiled in black, being admitted.

The undertaker spoke in sepulchral tones, 'Mrs Grantham, I will leave you with the deceased for a few minutes if that is your wish?'

'Thank you, sir,' she replied. 'Yes, I must pay my respects.'

As he crept away and silently closed the door, she moved toward the sarcophagus and, raising her veil, peered within.

After a few seconds she spoke, very softly, but audibly enough for us to hear. 'Well, George, who would have thought that you would have gone to meet your maker before me? I can't pretend that I was very fond of you, but I'm sorry that you are no more. I believe you mentioned once that you would remember me in your will. I don't imagine it is anything much and I never expected to see the day when I might inherit. Anyway, we shall see. God bless you, George!'

The woman dropped her veil again, turned and left the apartment. Holmes and I held whispered converse concerning what we had heard and seen.

'She did not appear to be a suspect, Holmes.'

'Indeed, Watson, but she benefits from his will. I am already all but certain who is the guilty person and this episode is just to prove my theory.'

Perhaps another five or six minutes passed before a second person was ushered in; a man, perhaps in his early thirties, not in mourning attire and showing signs of having been fetched rather hurriedly, to judge by his unkempt hair and the state of his cravat.

He had a shocked, earnest expression and spoke rather shakily. 'George, oh George, old man! How could fate be so unkind as to strike you down in your prime and at the very height of your talented powers? Why, you look just like you once did when I saw you dozing in your dressing-room between houses.'

Evidently devout, the man bowed his head in prayer, and I could not catch his words.

Then he raised his head and spoke again, 'God rest you, George. You will never be forgotten by your public, or by your old pal, Joe; oh, how I wish you had not promised me that stick-pin with the rubies. I will never be able to wear it without wishing you were still with us. I know you said it was valuable, but it is nothing like as valuable as your friendship. So long, old pal!'

He made a sad and silent exit. The next visitor was an attractive woman in a black dress with leg-of-mutton sleeves. She wore a black hat but I reckoned that it had not been made for mourning occasions despite the black, bird of paradise plumes which decorated it.

She sank onto her knees beside the coffin and spoke very quietly so that it was all we could do to hear her voice. 'Oh, Georgie, darling, it's Mavis Love. I know it's been a long time, but well, to be honest I've never been quite the same since that week in Glasgow when we were on the bill together. Those glorious afternoons at my hotel, and those late suppers at Ferguson's after the performances! Oh, I know we are both happily married now, George, but well, admit it, it's not quite the same, is it? We were young, we were happy, we were in love. I'll never forget you, darling. God bless you . . .'

She leaned over and kissed the reclining Robey on the forehead before she arose and departed tearfully.

As she left I whispered a question. 'He remembered her in his will?'

'Yes, Watson, after many years since their meeting. He must, indeed, have been in love with her. But I do not suspect the lady, as I believe her to be unaware of being mentioned in his will. Ah, but wait, we have another visitor . . .'

The undertaker was ushering in a tall, lean man with

homely features. I reckoned him to be about five and twenty, and not especially prosperous if his garments were anything to go by. He had a rather hangdog air of sadness until the undertaker had departed. He crossed to the coffin and had quite a lot to say.

The words he spoke were surprising, to say the least. 'So there you are cousin; yes, it's your dutiful cousin here, but I've not come to weep any crocodile tears. I don't know how you managed it, but you saved me a lot of hard work; you were supposed to meet your maker tomorrow night, second house. You would have gone out in style too, instead of at a first house, which is a bit poor for a star like you.'

Then his voice became sarcastic in the extreme.

'Still done up like a dog's dinner, eh? I bet you'll get a real all-star funeral, with all the big knobs of the theatre to see you off! Now, I know you haven't left me any sponduliks, you old skinflint, but you did assure me that I could have those bloomin' old violins that you spent so much time making. Well, no one will know that the Gelado copy in your workshop is the real thing! I'll leave it a month or two — not too long, in case they discover that the one at the museum is really your copy — then I'll dirty it up a bit and "discover" it in a junk shop. Well, that's my story. I shall get thousands for it. It was so easy, except that you had to be dead! Well, now it's all right, I'll say it is! I was getting heartily sick of having to sneak into that dome at Murphy's so that I could plan your demise. I tried the sandbag and missed; yes, and missed with the knife too. That was a close call. It's a good job that I had rigged that pulley to take me back into the dome while the lights were out. Just think,

I'm the man who fooled Sherlock Holmes. But then it is all over now, I'll not be bothered with him any more. Fate intervened and I won't have to see your ugly old face any more, either with or without that muck that you slap onto it, will I? Everyone used to taunt me, "Why aren't you clever like your cousin?" Well, I am clever, extremely clever, even if fate did finish the job for me!'

At this point, dear reader, something happened which made everything which had already amazed me sink into a state of mediocrity. I had just heard Charles Robey, George's cousin, admit, albeit quietly, that he had been the would-be assassin, and more, that he had burgled both the Museum of Stringed Masterpieces and George's workshop in order to exchange the copy for the real Gelado, knowing that the real instrument, still thought to be the copy, would become his, quite legally. That he had used the top of the theatre, a false dome, never visited, as the headquarters from which to carry out his ghastly scheme to kill his cousin, had also amazed me. But what happened next brought me near to swooning for only the second time in my life.

My eyes did not deceive me. George Robey suddenly reared up from his coffin to a seated position and wrapped his white-gloved hands around Charles Robey's throat!

Robey's rich voice suddenly and loudly erupted, 'You wretched, ungrateful, evil creature . . . oh, viper in my bosom, I intend to tear you limb from limb!'

Holmes urgently drew aside the draperies and shouted to Robey, 'Robey, have a care! You have played your part well and we have the admission we were seeking. Do not compromise yourself, leave him to the authorities!'

The eminent comedian took Holmes's hint and, despite his towering rage, slackened his hold upon the throat of his cousin, Charles. I noticed that, as I helped Robey out of his premature coffin, Holmes placed himself between Charles Robey and the door. But the would-be assassin showed no sign of attempting to flee. He had, of course, received a very great shock in seeing the apparent rising from the dead of his cousin, but was regaining his nerve, of which he evidently had quite a lot.

He turned to address my friend. 'Very clever, Mr Detective! So, you discovered my eyrie and dropped a sandbag, eh? Well, you must have done it very skilfully. It is sometimes more difficult to make a deliberate miss than to find your target; aye, even when the victim is a knowing and willing participant. Well, you fooled me, especially when George suddenly came back to life. But you know, it is all to no avail. It is true I have lost the Gelado which I worked so hard to make legally mine, but at least I retain my freedom for you cannot restrain me, and I don't believe the authorities will accept the so-called confession for I shall deny everything. Now stand aside for I wish to leave, and you cannot stop me!'

'No, Mr Charles Robey? But I can, and I arrest you upon a charge of attempted murder, and the theft from a museum of a valuable antique violin!'

Yet another shock had been delivered, making your humble scribe reel with astonishment for perhaps the third, or was it fourth, time within the hour. Yes, the voice was indeed familiar, and so was the sight of Inspector Lestrade of Scotland Yard as he emerged from the curtained alcove opposite to the one that Holmes and I had used as a 'hide'. Moreover, he was not alone, having a police constable with him who duly apprehended and handcuffed the hapless rascal.

'Oh, Mr Holmes, you surpass yourself!' The mockery in Charles Robey's voice showed that he was game to the last, showing no remorse.

As the constable took Charles away, George Robey started to strip away his comic neckpiece and to dab his brow with a handkerchief.

He had regained his composure and pleaded to be taken home that he might remove his motley. 'I mean to say, it has been quite a night, gentlemen. Just look at my handkerchief . . . finest Irish linen, cost me five and nine and now it is covered with the same!'

Holmes chuckled, for he alone among us understood Robey's 'joke'. As we strolled out to take Lestrade's carriage back to Robey's home he quietly explained, 'You see, Watson, a comedian usually makes his face up with a groundwork of colour produced by mixing two sticks of makeup, numbers "five" and "nine". Robey would have us believe that the handkerchief cost him "five and nine" in shillings and pence.'

I understood, but could not find it dreadfully funny, however, for I had received so many shocks as to make it difficult for my sense of humour to operate.

Holmes patted me on the shoulder. 'My dear Watson, never mind, for it is an actor's joke. You have often said that I should have been an actor, which is possibly why I find it amusing?'

*

Mrs Robey greeted us without any show of surprise or relief, for Robey and my friend had made sure that no word of the false demise should reach her. Of course, she was undismayed by the sudden appearance of guests at midnight, for she was the wife of a professional variety artiste. She soon busied herself in fetching tasty cold cuts and steaming coffee. Then, like a dutiful and diplomatic wife, she excused herself and went to her bed.

Needless to say, the events of the evening occupied our conversation into the small hours of the morning.

Holmes began with an apology. 'My dear Watson, first let me apologise for not letting you in on the little plot which Mr Robey and I concocted. But you see, I relied upon your reactions to the news of our friend's exaggerated demise being the right ones. You are not much of an actor as you have often yourself remarked. Moreover, I did genuinely require your assistance in the matter of the Reigate errand.'

I shrugged. It was not the first time that Holmes had dealt me this particular card. For, had he not kept me at Dartmoor, sending written reports to Baker Street when he was himself hiding out on the moors, fully aware of what was going on? Then, more recently, he had spent several years keeping me in the belief that he was dead consequent upon a fall from an Alpine place. He called me his best, nay, only friend, yet time and again he felt that he could not take me completely into his confidence. Ah well, despite this shortcoming in his friendship, he remained the finest man that I had ever known.

It was not long before George Robey rejoined us, having

taken the opportunity to wash and change. He looked comfortable now in his silk dressing-robe.

He, of course, had been completely in Holmes's confidence and apologised to me, saying, 'Your amazement was little short of that displayed by my wretched cousin. I was never so surprised as when Holmes told me of his findings in that direction. There was a man I had always respected even if he was not a man to whom one could become close. I did always sense a little envy in his make up. He tried to become a variety artiste himself once, billing himself as "Charles, the cousin of George Robey"! It was presented on the posters as if I might myself be part of the show. I didn't worry about it myself, but my agent was furious, took out a writ and a magistrate forbade my cousin to repeat the billing. Well, gentlemen, he changed it, and do you know what he changed it to?'

We shook our heads and he carried on, 'He billed himself as "Charles, formerly the cousin of George Robey"! Would you credit his nerve?'

We laughed, because it was extremely funny, but I was not too sure if we could completely believe it. After all, Robey was a comedian!

It was Lestrade who brought us all down to earth again. 'For attempting to steal the Gelado he would get five years,' he said, 'but attempted murder is another thing. I think he will be quite an old man before he is at liberty.'

George Robey frowned, 'I say, Inspector, do you think we need to charge him with that? I mean, surely five years behind bars is enough of a lesson for anyone.'

The inspector was none too pleased with this suggestion, but Holmes nodded. 'Perhaps something can be salvaged from this seeming wreck of an individual. It would indeed be generous and forgiving of you to not pursue that matter. It is something between yourself and your conscience.'

I remember thinking what a kindly and very likeable man Robey was. But I felt that the subject should be left, for the moment, and raised a fresh question. 'Holmes, how did you gain admission to the false theatre dome?'

'Very easily, Watson, I discovered the all but forgotten fire escape ladder on the far side of the building. Charles Robey had discovered it long before and that space betwixt dome and false top provided a haven for his wickedness. He had found the long-neglected sliding panel and its control. Through that aperture he could drop counterweights, even sneak out into the dim flies and cause a drop-scene to fall; he was even able to drop, on one occasion, into the wings to throw a knife and return to the roof within seconds, aided by the darkness and an ingenious pulley attached to a belt at his waist. It worked rather like that used by the fairy in a pantomime. A spring winch would whisk him away, operated by a sharp tug on the wire that supported him.'

It was perhaps three of the clock when I suggested the possibility of returning to Baker Street. This entailed Lestrade taking us in the police carriage, rather than our chancing the discovery of a passing hansom. I thought, when we had bade the inspector goodnight, that it was only the matter of a few minutes before I could gratefully sink my head upon my pillow. It had been a long day, with more shocks and surprises than, I felt, were good for me. But another was to greet us!

As we climbed the stairs I fancied that I heard the yapping of a dog from within our rooms. I could not believe it to be so, knowing of Holmes's extreme dislike of canines, save those of the useful working variety. That yap could scarcely have been uttered by a bloodhound.

As we opened the door to our apartments we were greeted by a most dreadful sight, a really ghastly little pug-dog was leaping around and had an object in its mouth which looked suspiciously like one of Holmes's favourite calabashes!

The basket, which I had brought back from Reigate, stood open on what was left of Mrs Hudson's carpet and we spent a quarter of an hour catching the wretched creature and returning it to the basket. There was a note from Mrs Hudson pinned to the lid:

Dear Doctor,
I have had your basket and occupant in my kitchen as long as I could stand it. What is it, some sort of banshee?

Yours respectfully,
Mrs H. Hudson

'I suppose she put the basket here and the wretched thing managed to escape.' I spoke the obvious.

Once the animal had been captured, Holmes seemed resigned to its presence and its yapping. 'So it would seem, Watson. I know you have suffered through it, but just think how Mrs Beadle will beam at you when she learns how you fearlessly retrieved her pug-dog?'

'It was not I who recovered it, Holmes. I merely conveyed it from Reigate.'

'Quite so, but I will not say a word!'

I glared at him, 'Irony does not suit you, Holmes!'

CHAPTER SIX

Finale at Murphy's

I considered that I was entitled to sleep late and gave no apology for my late appearance at breakfast. The pug was still yapping and wearily, purely for reasons of humanity, I released it and gave it food and drink. A sausage, some bacon and a dish of milk and water. When a visitor arrived and proved to be Mrs Beadle herself, I heaved a sigh of relief.

Holmes seemed able to ignore everything save the necessary negotiations. 'My dear lady, pray enter and take a seat; you will find this one the most comfortable. See how well your little friend has been cared for! My friend and colleague, Dr John Watson, has only just finished feeding him with tender morsels from his own plate.'

Mrs Beadle, a huge, fur-coated and ostrich-feather-hatted woman, fawned upon me. 'Dr Watson, how kind you are. I can see you just love little doggies! See how merrily he is playing with that slipper; what is that substance that is falling from it?'

I smiled glassily as I rescued Holmes's tobacco and the Turkish slipper which normally housed it. I managed to grab the little dog as gently as I could and handed it to the woman who nursed it like a child.

'Oh, see how happy he is at being rescued from his wicked abductor by the intrepid Mr Holmes! Say "thank you" to Mr Holmes, Binkie.'

She thrust the dog at Holmes's face and he managed to avoid damage to his prominent nose very narrowly indeed. She left with Binkie in his basket, a very satisfied customer.

'As a matter of interest, how did you find the dog, Holmes?'

'I didn't, Flood found it. He finds all the lost dogs for me, he has underworld connections with people who abduct dogs. Her fee will more than pay the ransom, and the whole matter is out of my way.'

'So you did nothing save pay a ransom?'

'It was the easiest and quickest way. Had I called it a ransom she might have had to battle with her conscience, but a fee for my services she would pay no matter how high it might seem.'

'I thought you never varied your charge save where you omitted it entirely?'

Holmes smiled enigmatically. 'My dear fellow, some rules were made to be broken!'

The silence in the rooms was golden, so I had to agree with him. He informed me that our next step was to accompany George Robey to the Museum of Stringed Masterpieces, in order to return their Gelado. At eleven of the clock Robey duly arrived carrying a violin-case. He was spruce and jaunty, with no suggestion of lost slumber.

When I remarked upon this, he replied, 'My dear doctor, I am a performer and we cat-nap, rather than sleep. We are creatures of the night, like detectives, I mean to say!'

Holmes smiled grimly at this comparison, and I had to admit that Holmes also looked bright enough. We sent Billy for a hansom and made our way south of the river.

The curator was pleased enough to see us, but did not unbend to the extent of offering any sort of thanks for the safe return of his precious Gelado.

Moreover, he examined both instruments again very carefully indeed before he agreed finally to the exchange. 'Really, Mr Robey, if you must make such exact replicas you might at least mark them in some way, making their origin beyond doubt.' The officious man spoke petulantly.

The comedian was never stuck for an answer. 'Perhaps I'll stick to making 'cellos. It would make an exchange rather more obvious and difficult.'

At this point we left feeling that we had done all that we could. Holmes's parting shot was to suggest an attendant be stationed near the Gelado at all times. For two seconds I felt that the ungrateful curator might thank Holmes for the suggestion. It was foolish of me.

'Well, my dear Robey, I think that all is put to rights now. Your would-be assassin is in prison — by the way, don't forget to make a new will — Murphy's ghost has been laid, and Mrs Beadle has got her Binkie back!'

I suppressed a smile, thinking that Holmes had made it all sound like the final lines of a pantomime. I felt like adding, 'The babes have been found, King Richard is home from the Crusades and Robin has been made Earl of Huntingdon!', but I thought better of it. Holmes has a sense of humour, but not of the ridiculous.

That night, to my amazement, Holmes suggested a visit to the House on the Green!

'I would have thought you had indulged my tastes a little more than your generosity demanded.'

'Oh, I don't know, Watson. I am becoming quite fond of the Varieties. In any case, friend Robey has booked a box for us and is making it quite an occasion.'

Old Murphy seemed quite glad to see us as we presented our special tickets. 'Given up going in on your "Wilkies", then?' The performance, although by now familiar to us, seemed different for two reasons. We were seeing the final performance of the week and viewing it from a completely different angle. Looking down from a stage box is rather different from viewing the performance looking upwards from the stalls. Neither is it quite the same as viewing from the balcony above because the stage box is so close that one can see the bald spot on a performer's head. During the interval Murphy stood us champagne in the stalls bar.

I looked around for Robey but Holmes explained his absence to me. 'He will be on stage within half-an-hour or so, and will, by now, be in full makeup and costume. You know by now that it is strictly forbidden for a performer to be seen in the auditorium in his motley.'

Murphy smiled approvingly.

'Does this even apply to the top of the bill?' I asked.

'Especially the top of the bill,' Murphy explained, 'for he, or she, is expected to provide a good example to the "wines and spirits".'

Even Holmes was puzzled by this expression, 'The "wines and spirits"?'

The showman explained. 'It is an old music-hall expression dating from a time when the theatres were little more than public houses with a few turns. The programmes would prominently display the names of the star artistes, but the others would be printed small, in type that was the same size as that advertising wines and spirits.'

Suddenly the bell rang and we made our way back to the box. The turns that we already knew so well appeared, yet all seemed to work with an added zest. Then, when it was Robey's turn, we could tell that something special was to be expected. Old Murphy, himself, walked out onto the stage with great aplomb and to considerable applause.

He held up his hands to beg for a hearing. 'Ladies and gentlemen. Some of you may have heard rumours concerning the strange events that have dogged our efforts to entertain you this week. Someone has been trying to harm our dear friend and top of the bill, George Robey!'

There were cries of 'Shame!' and 'Good old George!'

'But I am delighted to be able to announce that due to the efforts of a certain notable gentleman, himself a celebrity, the assailant has been captured and put in chokey where he belongs.'

More cheers and shouts.

'Let me introduce that famous gentleman to whom we owe the safety of our George, Mr Sherlock Holmes!'

A spotlight was shone upon the box and Holmes seemed quite embarrassed, especially when there were cries of 'Speech!' He waved his hands but sat down.

Murphy continued his speech. 'I'm going to ask all of you to join the gentlemen of the orchestra in a chorus of "For He's a Jolly Good Fellow" as we welcome your friend and mine, Mr George Robey!'

The band went into a spirited rendition of the named ditty as Murphy retired to one wing of the proscenium and George Robey entered from the other. He was thrown a little bit, I thought, through not hearing his usual music, but very quickly recovered his usual composure.

'I mean to say, let there be melody within reason, but modulate your cantatas with a modicum of ta ra ra boom de ay! Only last evening I stood upon this spot when someone tried to decapitate me with a sandbag, they did really. I'd rather go to Brighton for that sort of thing. Last time I went to Brighton it was for the races. I've been going there since Big Ben was a little watch. A woman rattled a tin under my nose and asked if I would like to support lame animals. I told her I put all my money on one in the three-thirty.'

Yes, George Robey was 'away' as it is known at Murphy's. He sang comic songs that I had not heard him sing before and told crisp new jokes, like a man reborn. Perhaps it was his recent misadventures and their happy culmination which gave him this extra zest. Of course by the time he had finished he had well overplayed his time and the audience should by then have been on their way home, whistling the songs they had heard and reminding each other of the merry quips and the feats of skill that they had been witness to. But tonight, it seemed, was a special night, and only a tiny handful, who were expected at home, left the theatre and there were the raucous cries of 'encore' and 'give us another one, George!' Eventually, having occupied quite double his allocated time upon the stage, Robey held up his hands as if in surrender.

When he started his speech you could have heard a pin drop. 'Ladies and gentlemen, I have been your red-nosed funnyman for quite a number of years and I mean to go on being just that until you consider me to be an old retainer. I appreciate your happiness at my close call, and feel that I should return the kindness by bringing you something really special. Older patrons will easily remember a protean artiste who called himself Castelli.'

There were a few cries of 'Yes . . . very well!'

'Well, you haven't been seeing him for a long time because he has been on an extended world tour. Now why, you might ask, would such a great performer want to stay away from his native land for so long? Well, I'll tell you why; about ten years ago Castelli had prepared a new act which was to have been even greater than the one for which he was famous, and he chose this very theatre at which to present its première. Unfortunately, some evil person, or persons, who had better stay unknown, organised a claque — you know, all of you, what that is. Yes, but this was not a claque to applaud the artiste, but to boo and ridicule him! (Cries of 'shame') I know you, the patrons of Murphy's, well enough to be sure that none of you were involved. So I have implored Castelli to come back and give us another chance. I'm sure you will show your appreciation for — Castelli!'

Robey made his exit, and the lights dimmed, to rekindle and reveal a scene representing the interior of a poor cottage where the female figure of Nancy held forth to the hidden Bill Sykes who was evidently behind a screen. She went behind the screen and it seemed that immediately Bill Sykes himself, with his staved-in hat and ragged rainment emerged. The audience could not believe that it was the same person, and later, when Bill Sykes went out through a door and Fagin entered almost at once through the window, those who had not seen Castelli before realised that they were witness to something quite unbelievable in the quick-change line.

The applause when Castelli came out before the curtain to take his call was quite deafening, and to thunderous shouts of 'speech . . . speech!', the tears ran down his face. His hands shook, not from stage fright or palsy, but from delighted reaction to the admiration and affection shown him by the audience.

He spoke, quaveringly at first, but as he continued, he gained in oratorial strength. 'Ladies and gentlemen, my dear friends, I have to thank you for having me back. I was wronged, yet I was also wrong, for I should have faced the music all those years ago and carried on, as I intend doing now, if anyone will have me! But I want you to know that I have George Robey and one other man to thank for this change back to the right direction . . . Mr Sherlock Holmes! I would beg you to rise and join me in singing "For He's a Jolly Good Fellow"!'

The band again struck up this chorus but this time it was Holmes who was the touched and honoured one. As he stood with bared head, I believe he was happy in the adulation of the crowd.

Epilogue at Baker Street

An amazing talent of my friend, Sherlock Holmes, is his ability to finish with a project, utterly and completely, as soon as his own part in it has been played. As his Boswell I, of course, tend to make notes for the future documentation of his cases, but he has always been singularly uninterested in what has been or what might be. He lives for the present, and if there is nothing to presently interest him, he is apt to fall prey to those vices which so afflicted him during one period of his life. I was, therefore, glad to know that his services were still so much in demand when the matter had been concluded at the House on the Green and its hauntings, so entirely connected with the case of George Robey's violin which had so closely resembled the priceless Gelado. I had a presentiment that Robey might present Holmes with one of his beautifully made instruments, each a copy of an old master. Perhaps the knowledge that my friend already owned a Stradivarius stopped him from doing so.

Instead, a special messenger arrived, within a few days of the termination of the affair, bearing gifts of a rather different sort. For Holmes there were cigars, of a rare Cuban make, housed, not in a box, but in a beautifully made miniature copper coal-scuttle! My own gift was one of these patent clocks which arouse the sleeper at a predetermined hour. Robey is, to my mind, that rarity: a comedian with a sense of humour.

Thanks to the noisy little timepiece, I had soon all but forsaken my bad habit of late rising. There even came a morning when I beat Holmes to the breakfast table. He laughed at my ironic reversal of the usual situation.

'Upon my word, Watson, I trust you are not going to make a habit of ruining my best criticism of your character! You know we are not engaged upon anything unduly urgent at present.'

I grunted and passed him the kidneys. 'You know, Holmes, I had not realised that I had been missing the best of Mrs Hudson's delicacies. By the way, all the details concerning the mysteries at the House on the Green are clear to me save one.'

'Oh, really Watson, pray tell me if I have overlooked some detail in the summing-up which I provided for Robey and Inspector Lestrade.'

'Well, this would not concern the inspector because I believe you were kind enough to leave out most of Castelli's playing of the ghost in your official reports.'

'Quite so, the protean artiste had suffered enough and done no real harm.'

'Exactly, but what was the source of the apparition that was seen by a couple of patrons at the hall whilst Castelli was actually performing?'

'I did hear something of that, but then the sort of patron that was not sitting in his seat at that point, Watson, would probably have been emerging from the stalls bar, and who can say what apparitions would be seen by a topper who would miss seeing George Robey and Castelli?'

'Holmes, is that a serious deduction?'

'No, Watson, but it is the best effort I can make before I have had my breakfast, and short of ruining your impression that I have no belief in the supernatural.'

'Holmes, I wish I had not raised the subject.'

If my snappish remark had not stopped the conversation, the next event most certainly would have done so. For there was a knock upon the door followed by the sounds made by Mrs Hudson descending the stairs and then returning, unaccompanied by a visitor, after a rather lengthy period.

As her steps were heard, Holmes said, 'I wonder if Mrs Hudson bears more gifts from admiring clients?'

'What makes you think that?'

'The caller was a messenger delivering something. His knock had not the irreverence of some butcher's-boy, nor yet that tentative touch of a prospective client. This was the knock of a messenger with a package, if I am not mistaken.'

'Why not an envelope?'

'No, Watson, Mrs Hudson's return is sufficiently delayed in its style and timing to suggest that she is carrying something, carefully.'

As if to bolster his deduction, Mrs Hudson was heard to deposit an object upon the floor that she might have a free hand to knock.

'Dr Watson, there is a delivery for you, and I don't much like the look or sound of it!'

She ducked out of sight, then returned, bearing a box which required both her hands to carry. The box had a number of holes punched into its heavy cardboard; the good lady put it down on the floor, gratefully ridding herself, I felt, of its cumbersome size rather than any great weight. She had a lavender blue envelope in her belt which she whipped out and handed to me. After she had left, I studied the envelope which was addressed to me in a stylish feminine hand.

I turned to Holmes and said, 'I know your methods and I will apply them. The gift is from Mrs Robey in gratitude for my own small role in the affair of the violin. Flowers are a strange gift for a woman to give to a man, but the airholes tell their own story. Strange that Mrs Robey should send me flowers.'

'You are assuming far too much, Watson; you assume that the box contains flowers, and you assume that they are from Mrs Robey.'

'You think otherwise?'

'Certainly, flowers are not alone in requiring airholes in their container, and Mrs Robey is not the only woman in the world!'

'The only woman that I can think of at the moment likely to send me a gift.'

'You underestimate your charms as usual, Watson; moreover, you are forever performing good deeds, most of which you instantly forget. Take your recent excursion to the wilds of Surrey.'

'You mean fetching that dog back from Reigate for your lady client?'

'Oh come, Watson, she was more than just my lady client, for was she not the owner of the lost pug-dog? "Binkie" I seem to remember the revolting little creature was called. Mrs Beadle took quite a liking to you and who knows what you might find lurking in that box!'

I was by now uneasy, and in my irritation I snapped, 'Holmes, sarcasm does not become you . . .'

He laughed and bade me read aloud the letter.

'Having, of course, perused it and assured yourself that it is fit for my tender ears.'

In my frustration with his irony, I tore open the envelope and read the letter aloud without pausing to assure myself regarding its content:

My dear Dr Watson,
Just a little gift to show my appreciation of your kindness in playing such a big part in the return to me of my beloved Binkie.

I could not help but notice how very attached to you he had become, and I feel sure the feeling was returned by your good self. Well, dear Dr Watson, you are in luck! You see, Binkie's mate, Flossie, has recently produced six adorable puppies. I could not think of a better gift than one of them to someone as kindly as yourself, or a better home for Susie. She is nine weeks old and will be no trouble at all for you to keep once you have finished her house-training. Be sure she is fed three times a day, on minced beef and well-broken dog meal, and a dish of turtle soup last thing at night. Brush her daily and keep a dish of clean water available for her at all times. She will need to be taken for a little walk five times a day;

early morning (about seven), then after each meal and, of course, last thing at night . . .'

'Watson, pray cease reading, I have no more time to listen to such prattle. Just take my advice and get rid of the creature without even opening the box. Remember the damage that the infamous Binkie caused. If Mrs Hudson learns that you are planning to keep a dog she will throw us both out, after that last episode. Just return the box to its sender and remember that there is work for us to do.'

I was opening the box as I asked, 'What work? Why, I thought you were marking time, waiting for new cases?'

'Well, that is true,' he grunted, 'but I have a feeling that something very important is about to turn up.'

'Holmes, you are beginning to sound like Micawber. See, here is Susie and a delightful little creature she is, too.'

As I lifted the tiny pug-dog out of the box, straw scattered onto the carpet to my friend's annoyance, but I realised that this was as nothing compared to the form that his future tempers would take if I accepted the gift. But how could one return the delightful little animal without causing offence to the lady? However, my salvation was at hand, though I could not know it at the time.

This salvation came in the unlikely form of Billy, the page. Billy had been there in the background these many years, very useful when there were errands to be run and cabs to be called; and, doubtless, very useful to Mrs Hudson in the kitchen. Of course, I knew in my heart that it was impossible for the same Billy to have been page-boy at 221B for so long unless his growth had been well and truly stunted (even then there would have been other signs of ageing), but I had always been willing to treat him as if he were the same boy. I am convinced that Holmes, although so shrewd of mind, had never given this matter thought, quite ignoring the illogicality of a page-boy who never aged, and the matter was never discussed. Wherever Mrs Hudson got them from, they seemed to be from a mould. However, whoever this particular Billy was, he quite saved me from a tricky situation. He had entered to deliver a message to Holmes and, as my friend scrutinised it, he sank to his knees to play with Susie, enraptured with the little creature.

'Pug-dog, ain't she?'

'Yes, Billy, do you like her?'

'Why, yes, doctor, I'm very fond of dogs.'

A wicked scheme was beginning to form itself in my mind. 'What would you say if I could get you one like this at no cost?'

'What? Why she's a pedigree. I know, because my uncle has a pug and he is lookin' for one to be its mate, but he can't afford it just yet. I go to stay there every few weeks for a day or two. As a matter of fact I'm off there today, until next Monday. But I could not keep one of these myself, not here: Mrs Hudson would go frantic!'

'But what if you were to keep him at your uncle's place? She could be your dog, but a companion to the one he has at the same time.'

'Golly, do you mean that I can have this one?'

He took the wriggling tiny pug into his arms, obviously delighted.

'She is yours, if you will take her now, care for all her needs and transport her to your uncle's place forthwith!'

The boy was delighted and so was I, and proud of myself for having so craftily resolved the situation. In my mind I was already composing a letter of thanks to Mrs Beadle, including the words . . . 'It would be unfair to keep her cooped up at Baker Street, but a colleague will keep her for me somewhere more suitable where she will have the companionship of another of her kind. I shall, of course, keep in touch with her situation and be sure that she is well-cared for . . .' etc.

Holmes looked up from the message that he had been reading, seemingly completely preoccupied. He surprised me, therefore, when he said, 'Watson, I congratulate you upon handling a very tricky situation admirably. By the way, the actual director of the Museum of Stringed Masterpieces has written me a letter of gratitude for the way in which I handled the Gelado situation. Evidently the episode could not, after all, be kept a secret from him. He has, however, had a rather novel version of the facts from his curator in which that worthy appears to have himself noticed the change in the instrument and dealt with the matter so responsibly, using his initiative in calling upon my services! Ah well, good luck to him if he has convinced those over him of that. Oh, by the way, he has sent me a quite generous cheque, and despite my ethics in that direction, I am inclined to keep it.'

We settled to take coffee and, as he poured, Holmes added, 'You know, Watson, quite a lot that was both stimulating and profitable emerged from your choice of entertainment.'

I said nothing, not wishing to contradict him by saying that he had himself made the suggestion that we might go to the House on the Green.

Then he made a further addendum. 'Where shall we go this evening, Watson, Murphy's, the Met or some other palace of varieties?'

But I quickly shook my head and said, 'Your turn to choose, Holmes. How about the Royal Albert Hall? Who knows, we might be able to get in on our "Wilkies"!'